William Blaikie

How to Get Strong and How to Stay So

outlook

William Blaikie

How to Get Strong and How to Stay So

1st Edition | ISBN: 978-3-75238-293-8

Place of Publication: Frankfurt am Main, Germany

Year of Publication: 2020

Outlook Verlag GmbH, Germany.

Reproduction of the original.

HOW TO GET STRONG

AND

HOW TO STAY SO
BY
WILLIAM BLAIKIE

PREFACE.

MILLIONS of our people pass their lives in cities and towns, and at work which keeps them nearly all day in-doors. Many hours are devoted for days and years, under careful teachers, and many millions of dollars are spent annually, in educating the mind and the moral nature. But the body is allowed to grow up all uneducated; indeed, often such a weak, shaky affair that it gets easily out of order, especially in middle and later life, and its owner is wholly unequal to tasks which would have proved easy to him, had he given it even a tithe of the education bestowed so generously in other directions. Not a few, to be sure, have the advantage in youth of years of active out-door life on a farm, and so lay up a store of vigor which stands them in good stead throughout a lifetime. But many, and especially those born and reared in towns and cities, have had no such training, or any equivalent, and so never have the developed lungs and muscles, the strong heart and vigorous digestion—in short, the improved tone and strength in all their vital organs— which any sensible plan of body-culture, followed up daily, would have secured. It does not matter so much whether we get vigor on the farm, the deck, the tow-path, or in the gymnasium, if we only get it. Fortunately, if not gotten in youth, when we are plastic and easily shaped, it may still be had, even far on in middle life, by judicious and systematic exercise, aimed first to bring up the weak and unused parts, and then by general work daily which shall maintain the equal development of the whole.

The aim here has been, not to write a profound treatise on gymnastics, and point out how to eventually reach great performance in this art, but rather in a way so plain and untechnical that even any intelligent boy or girl can readily understand it, to first give the reader a nudge to take better care of his body, and so of his health, and then to point out one way to do it. That there are a hundred other ways is cheerfully conceded. If anything said here should stir up some to vigorously take hold of, and faithfully follow up, either the plan here indicated or any one of these others, it cannot fail to bring them marked benefit, and so to gratify

THE AUTHOR.

New York, July, 1883.

2

CHAPTER I.
DO WE INHERIT SHAPELY BODIES?

PROBABLY more men walk past the corner of Broadway and Fulton Street, in New York city, in the course of one year, than any other point in America—men of all nations and ages, heights and weights. Look at them carefully as they pass, and you will see that scarcely one in ten is either erect or thoroughly well-built. Some slouch their shoulders and double in at the waist; some overstep; others cant to one side; this one has one shoulder higher than the other, and that one both too high; some have heavy bodies and light legs, others the reverse; and so on, each with his own peculiarities. A thoroughly erect, well-proportioned man, easy and graceful in his movements, is far from a frequent sight. Any one accustomed to athletic work, and knowing what it can do for the body, must at times have wondered why most men allowed themselves to go along for years, perhaps through life, so carrying themselves as not only to lack the outward grace and ease they might possess, and which they occasionally see in others, but so as to directly cramp and impede one or more of the vital organs.

Nor is it always the man's fault that he is ill-proportioned. In most cases it comes down from his progenitors. The father's walk and physical peculiarities appear in the son, often so plainly that the former's calling might almost be told from a look at the latter.

A very great majority of Americans are the sons either of farmers or merchants, mechanics or laborers. The work of each class soon develops peculiar characteristics. No one of the four classes has ordinarily had any training at all aimed to make him equally strong all over. Broad as is the variety of the farmer's work, far the greater, and certainly the heavier, part of it tends to make him stoop forward and become inerect. No man stands up straight and mows. When he shovels, he bends more yet; and every ounce of spade or load pulls him over, till, after much of this sort of work, it requires an effort to stand upright. Ploughing is better for the upper body, but it does not last long. While it keeps one walking over uneven ground, it soon brings on an awkward, clumsy step, raising, as it does, the foot unnaturally high. Chopping is excellent for the upper man, but does little for his legs. In hand-raking and hoeing the man may remain erect; but in pitching and building the load, in nearly every sort of lifting, and especially the heavier sorts, as in handling heavy stone or timber, his back is always bent over. It is so much easier to slouch over when sitting on horse-rake, mower, or harvester, that most persons do it.

Scarcely any work on a farm makes one quick of foot. All the long day, while some of the muscles do the work, which tends to develop them, the rest are untaxed, and remain actually weak. A farmer is seldom a good walker, usually hitching up if he has an errand to go, though it be scarce a mile away; and he is rarely a good runner. He is a hearty, well-fed man, not only because wholesome food is plenty, but because his appetite is sharp, and he eats with relish and zest. Naturally a man thinks that, when he eats and sleeps well, he is pretty healthy, and so he usually is; but when he is contented with this condition of things, he overlooks the fact that he is developing some parts of his body, and leaving others weak; that the warp he is encouraging in that body, by twice as much work for the muscles of his back as for those of the front of his chest, while it enlarges the former, often so as to even render it muscle-bound, actually contracts the latter, and hence gives less room for heart, lungs, stomach, and all the vital organs, than a well-built man would have. If a man should tie up one arm, and with the other steadily swing a smith's hammer all day, there is little doubt that he would soon have an excellent appetite and the sweet sleep of the laboring man. But in what shape would it leave him in a few years, or even in a few months? The work of the farmer, ill-distributed as to the whole man, leaves him as really one-sided as the former. It is in a lesser degree, of course, but still so evident that he who looks even casually may see it.

While the farmer's work makes a man hearty and well, though lumbering, it takes the spring out of him. The merchant is, physically, however, in a worse position. Getting to his work in boyhood, sticking to it as long as the busiest man in the establishment, his body often utterly unfit and unready for even half the strain it bears, he struggles on through the boy's duties, the clerk's, and the salesman's, till he becomes a partner; or perhaps he starts as entry-clerk, rises to be book-keeper, and then stays there. In many kinds of work he has been obliged to stand nearly all day, till his sides and waist could scarcely bear it longer, and he often breaks down under the ceaseless pressure. If his work calls him out much, he finds that the constant walking, with his mind on the stretch, and more or less worried, does not bring him that vigor he naturally looks for from so much exercise, and at night he is jaded and used up, instead of being fresh and hearty. When exceptional tension comes, and business losses or reverses make him anxious and haggard, there is little in his daily work which tends to draw him out of a situation that he could have readily and easily fitted himself to face, and weather too, had he only known how. To be sure, when he gets well on and better to do, he rides out in the late afternoon, and domestic and social recreation in the evening may tend to freshen him, and fit him for the next day's round; but, especially if he has been a strong young man, he finds that he is changed, and cannot work on as he used to do. His bodily strength and endurance are gone. The reason why is plain enough: when he was at his best, he was doing most work, and of the sort to keep him in good condition. Now there is nothing between rising and bedtime to build up any such strength, and he is fortunate if he retains even half of what he had. To be sure, he does not need the strength of a stalwart young farmer; but, could he have retained it, he would have been surprised, if he had taken sufficient daily exercise to regulate himself, how valuable it would have been in toning him up for the severer work and trial of the day. If, instead of the taxed and worn-out nerves, he could have had the feeling of the man of sturdy physique, who keeps himself in condition, who does not know what it is to be nervous, what a priceless boon it would have been for him!

Who does not know among his friends business men whose faces show that they are nearly all the time overworked; who get thin, and stay so; who look tired, and are so; who go on dragging along through their duties—for they are men made of the stuff which does the duty as it comes up, whether hard or easy? The noon meal is rushed through, perhaps when the brain is at white-heat. More is eaten, both then and in the evening, than will digest; and good as is the after or the before dinner ride, as far as it goes, it does not go far enough to make the digestion sure. Then comes broken sleep. The man waking from it is not rested, is not rebuilt and strong, and ready for the new day.

With many men of this kind—and all city men know they are well-nigh innumerable—what wonder is it that nervous exhaustion is so frequent among them, and that physicians who make this disorder a specialty often have all that they can do? One of the most noted of them, Dr. S. Weir Mitchell, of Philadelphia, in his valuable little book, "Wear and Tear; or, Hints for the Overworked," page 46, says: "All classes of men who use the brain severely, and who have also—and this is important—seasons of excessive anxiety or grave responsibility, are subject to the same form of disease; and this is why, I presume, that I, as well as others who are accustomed to encounter nervous disorders, have met with numerous instances of nervous exhaustion among merchants and manufacturers.

"My note-books seem to show that manufacturers and certain classes of railway officials are the most liable to suffer from neural exhaustion. Next to these come merchants in general, brokers, etc.; then, less frequently, clergymen; still less often, lawyers; and, more rarely, doctors; while distressing cases are apt to occur among the over-schooled young of both sexes."

And while the more active among business men run into this sort of danger, those less exposed to it still do little or nothing to give themselves sound, vigorous bodies, so as to gain consequent energy and health, and so they go through life far less efficient and useful men than they might have been. Hence their sons have to suffer. The boy certainly cannot inherit from the father more vigor and stamina than the latter has, however favored the mother may have been; so, unless the boy has some sort of training which builds him up, his father's weaknesses or physical defects are very likely to show in the son.

Nor do most classes of mechanics fare much better. Take the heavier kinds of skilled labor. The blacksmith rarely uses one of his hands as much as the other, especially in heavy work, and often has poor legs. Indeed, if he has good legs, he does not get them from his calling. The stone-mason is equally one-handed—one hand merely guiding a light tool, the other swinging a heavy mallet. Nine-tenths of all machinists are right-handed. And so on, through the long list of the various trades where severe muscular exertion is requisite, there is a similar uneven distribution of the work to the various parts of the body, the right arm generally getting the lion's share, the left but little, the back more than the chest—or, rather, than the front chest—and the legs having but passive sort of work at best. Puddlers and boiler-makers, plumbers and carpenters, coopers and smiths, shipwrights, carriage-makers, tinners, and all who follow trades calling for vigorous muscular action, not only constantly work one side more than the other, but many of their tools are made, purposely, right-handed, so that they could hardly use them with the left hand if they wanted to. As to those whose work is more delicate, saddlers and shoe-makers, mill-hands and compositors, wood-turners, tailors, jewellers and engravers, and nearly all the lighter craftsmen, learn their trade with one hand, and would never venture to trust any of its finer work to the other. In short, take the mechanic where you will, in the vast majority of instances his right arm and side are larger and stronger than his left, and quite as often his vocation does little or nothing to strengthen and develop his legs.

The fact that most of these men have active work for some of the muscles, with enough of it to insure a good appetite, combined with inherited vigor, makes them often hearty men, but it leaves them unequally developed. When they get into the gymnasium, they are usually lacking in that symmetry, ease, and erectness which they might all along have had, had they but used the means. The result, then, of overworking one part of the body at the expense of the other, especially in heavier mechanical labors, and of too little vigorous action in the lighter, tends to make the average workman more prone to disease. Were there uniform development, and that daily vigorous exercise which would stimulate the dormant parts of the man's body, it would add to his life and usefulness.

But how is it with the sturdy laborer? He can hardly be liable to the same defects. His work certainly must call into play every muscle of his body.

Well, watch him awhile and see. Try the coal-heaver. His surely is heavy, hard work, and must make him exert himself all over. But does it? While it keeps his knees steadily bent, his back is all the while over his work. The tons of coal he lifts daily with his shovel gradually, but with positive certainty, insures his back remaining somewhat bent when his work for the time is done. When a year is spent at such labor, the back must take a lasting curve. While his back broadens, growing thick and powerful, his chest does not get so much to do; hence he is soon a round-shouldered man. As he does not hold his chest out, nor his neck and head erect, he contracts his lung-room, as well, indeed, as his general vital-room. Scarce any man grows earlier muscle-bound, for few backs do so much hard work. Now, standing erect, let him try and slap the backs of his hands together behind his shoulders, keeping his arms horizontal and straight at the elbow. Now he will understand what is meant by being muscle-bound. It will be odd if he can get his hands within a foot of each other.

The navvy is no better. The gardener's helper has to do much stooping. So do track-hands, stone-breakers, truckmen, porters, longshoremen, and all the rest. Especially are ordinary day-laborers, whose tools are spade, pick, and bar, who are careless about their skin, who are exposed to dust and dirt, who are coarsely shod, most prone to have bad feet. They, too, have the hearty appetite and the sound sleep. Seldom do they give their bodily improvement a thought, and so often, like their own teeth, they decay before their time, and materially shorten their usefulness and their days.

Here, then, we see that the vast majority of men in this country—three out of four at least—are born of fathers but partially developed, and uniformly of inerect carriage.

And how is it with their mothers? Naturally they come, to a large extent, from the same classes. They inherit many of the characteristics of their fathers —size, color, temperament, and so on, and generally the same tendency to be stronger on one side than on the other. In the poorer classes their life is one of work, frequently of overwork and drudgery, and in ill-lighted, ill-ventilated apartments. Among those better off, they do not work enough, and often, though of vigorous parents, are not themselves strong.

Thoroughly healthy, hearty women are not common among us. Ask the family physician, and he will endorse this statement to an extent most men would not have supposed. American women are not good walkers. Look how they are astonished when they hear of some lady who walks from five to ten miles a day, and thinks nothing of it. One such effort would be positively dangerous to very many, indeed probably to the majority of our women, while nearly all of them would not get over its effects for several days. Yet many English and Canadian ladies take that much exercise daily from choice, and, finding the exhilaration, strength, and health it brings, and the general feeling of efficiency which it produces, would not give it up. No regular exercise is common among the great majority of the women of this country which makes them use both their hands alike, and is yet vigorous enough to add to the size and strength of their shoulders, chests, and arms. Ordinary house-work brings the hands of those who indulge in it a good deal to do, even though the washing and ironing are left to hired help. The care of children adds materially to the exertion called for in a day. But far too often both the house-work and the looking after the children are sources of great exertion. Were the woman strong and full of vigor, she would turn each off lightly, and still be fresh and hearty at the end of the day.

With the father, as with the mother, the conclusion arrived at seems to be as follows: now that the day's work is done, no matter whether it brings with it strength or weakness, let us be perfectly contented with things as they are. If it makes us one-handed, so be it. If it stoops the back over, so be it. If it does little or nothing for the lower limbs, or cramps the chest, or never half fills the lungs, or aids digestion not a whit, so be it. If it keeps some persons thin and tired-looking, and does not prevent others from growing too fleshy, it never occurs to most of them that a very small amount of knowledge and effort in the right direction would work wonders, and in a way which would be not only valuable but attractive.

Most of us get, then, from our parents a one-sided and partial development, and are contented with it. Unless we ourselves take steps to better our condition, unless we single out the weak spots, prescribe the work and the amount of it, and then do that work, we shall not remedy the evil. More than this, if we do not cure these defects, we will not only go through life with limited and cramped physical resources, with their accompanying disorders and ailments, but we will cruelly entail on our children defects and tendencies which might have readily been spared them, and for which they can fairly blame us. A little attention to the subject will show that the remedy is quite within our reach; and so plain is this, that a generation later, if the interest now awakening in this direction becomes, as it promises to, very general among us, our descendants will understand far better than we do that the body can be educated, as well as the mind or the moral nature; that, instead of interfering with the workings of these, the body will, when properly trained, directly and materially aid them; and, further, that there is no stand-point from which the matter can be viewed which will not show that such training will pay, and most handsomely at that.

CHAPTER II.

HALF-BUILT BOYS.

BUT, whatever our inherited lacks and strong points, few who have looked into the matter can have failed to notice that the popular sports and pastimes, both of our boyhood and youth, good as they are, as far as they go, are not in themselves vigorous enough, or well enough chosen to remedy the lack. The top, the marble, and the jack-knife of the boy are wielded with one hand, and for all the strength that wielding brings, it might as well have been confined to one. Flying kites is not likely to overdo the muscles. Yet top-time, marble-time, and kite-time generally cover all the available play hours of each day for a large portion of the year.

But he has more vigorous work than these bring. Well, what? Why, ball-playing and playing tag, and foot-ball, and skating, and coasting, and some croquet, and occasional archery, while he is a painfully accurate shot with a bean-shooter.

Well, in ball-playing he learns to pitch, to catch, to bat, to field, and to run bases. How many boys can pitch with either hand? Not one in a hundred, at least well enough to be of any use in a game. Observe the pitching arm and shoulder of some famous pitcher, and see how much larger they are than their mates. Dr. Sargent, for many years instructor in physical culture in Yale College, says that he has seen a well-known pitcher whose right shoulder was some two inches larger than the left; indeed, his whole right side seemed out of proportion with his left. The catcher draws both hands in toward him as the ball enters them, and passes it back to the pitcher almost always with the same hand. He has, in addition, to spring about on his feet, unless the balls come very uniformly, and to do much twisting and turning. The batter bats, not from either shoulder, but from one shoulder, to such an extent that those used to his batting know pretty well where he will knock the ball, though, did he bat from the other shoulder, the general direction of the knocking would be quite different. Some of the fielders have considerable running and some catching to do, and then to throw the ball in to pitcher, or baseman, or catcher. But that throw is always with the stronger hand, never with the other. Many of the fielders often have not one solitary thing to do but to walk to their stations, remain there while their side is out, and then walk back again, hardly getting work enough, in a cold day, to keep them warm. Running bases is sharp, jerky work, and a wretched substitute for steady, sensible running over a long distance. Nor is the fielder's running much better; and neither would ever teach a boy what he ought to know about distributing his strength in running, and how to get out of it what he readily might, and, more important yet, how to make himself an enduring long-distance runner. For all the work the former brings, ordinary, and even less than ordinary, strength of leg and lung will suffice, but for the latter it needs both good legs and good lungs.

Run most American boys of twelve or fourteen six or eight miles, or, rather, start them at it—let them all belong to the ball-nine if you will, too—and how many would cover half the distance, even at any pace worth calling a run? The English are, and have long been, ahead of us in this direction. To most readers the above distance seems far too long to let any boy of that age run. But, had he been always used to running—not fast, but steady running—it would not seem so. Tom Brown of Rugby, in the hares-and-hounds game, of which he gives us so graphic an account, makes both the hares and hounds cover a distance of nine miles without being much the worse for it, and yet they were simply school-boys, of all ages from twelve to eighteen.

Let him who thinks that the average American boy of the same age would have fared as well, go down to the public bath-house, and look carefully at a hundred or two of them as they tumble about in the water. He will see more big heads and slim necks, more poor legs and skinny arms, and lanky, half-built bodies than he would have ever imagined the whole neighborhood could produce. Or he need not see them stripped. One of our leading metropolitan journals, in an editorial recently, headed, "Give the boy a chance," said:

"About one in ten of all the boys in the Union are living in New York and the large cities immediately adjacent; and there are even more within the limits of Philadelphia, Boston, Chicago, and the other American cities whose population exceeds a hundred thousand. The wits of these millions of boys are being forced to their extreme capacity, whether they are taught in the school, the shop, or the street. But what is being done for their bodies? The answer may be obtained by standing at the door of almost any public or private school or academy at the hour of dismissal. *The inquirer will see a crowd of undersized, listless, thin-faced children, with scarcely any promise of manhood about them.*"

Take a tape-measure and get the girth of chest, upper and forearm, of waist, hips, thighs, and calves of these little fellows, likewise their heights and ages. Now send to England and get the statistics of the boys of the same age who are good at hares-and-hounds, at foot-ball, and see the difference. In every solitary measurement, save height, there is little doubt which would show the better figures. Even in height, it is more than probable that the article just quoted would find abundant foundation for calling our boys "undersized."

Next cross to Germany, and go to the schools where boys and their masters together, in vacation days, sometimes walk two or even three hundred miles, in that land where the far-famed German Turners, by long training, show a strength and agility combined which are astounding, and try the tape-measure there. Is there any question what the result would be? When the sweeping work the Germans made of it in their late war with France is called to mind, does it not look as if there was good ground for the assumption so freely made, that it was the superior physique of the Germans which did the business?

Where work is chosen that only sturdy limbs can do, and that work is gradually approached, and persistently stuck to, by-and-by the sturdy limbs come. But when all that these limbs are called on to do is light, spasmodic work, and there is none of the spur which youthful emulation and pride in superior strength bring, what wonder is it if the result is a weakly article?

Another and natural consequence many parents must have noticed. Often, in a city neighborhood, there is not one strong, efficient boy to lead on the rest, and show them the development which they might have and should have. Boys, like men, are fond of doing whatever they can do well, and of letting others see them do it, and, like their elders, they gladly follow a capable and self-reliant leader. But if no one of their number is equal to tasks which call for first-class strength and staying powers, when no one will lead the rest up to a higher physical plane, they never will get there.

It is not a good sign, or one that bodes well for our future, to see the play-grounds of our cities and towns so much neglected. You may stand on many of them for weeks together and not see one sharp, hot game of ball, or of anything else, where each contestant goes in with might and main, and the spectator becomes so interested as to hate to leave the fun. Foot-ball is a game as yet not at all general among us. Excellent is it for developing intrepidity and other manly qualities. The Duke of Wellington is reported to have said that her foot-ball fields were where England's soldiers were made. The short, hasty school recess in the crowded school-yard, or play snatched in the streets —these will never make robust and vigorous men. Yet these are too often all that our boys get, their cramped facilities for amusement soon bringing their natural result in small vital organs and half-developed limbs.

Many of our large cities are wretchedly off for play-grounds. Such open spaces as we have are fenced around, and have signs nailed all over them saying, "Keep off the grass!" at the same time forbidding games on the paths. One part of Boston Common used to be a famous play-ground; and many hard-fought battles has it seen at foot-ball, base-ball, hockey, and cricket. Many an active school-boy there has more than once temporarily bit the dust.

But now rows of street lamps run through that part of the Common, and the precious grass must be protected at all hazards. New York city is scarcely better off. Central Park, miles away from the great majority of the boys in the city, is elegant enough when they get to it; but let them once set their bounds and start a game of ball, or hares-and-hounds, or try a little jumping or running, on any one of those hundreds of beautiful acres, save in one solitary field, and see how soon the gray-coats will be upon them. The Battery, City Hall Park, Washington Square, Union Park, Stuyvesant Square, and Madison Square are well located, and would make capital play-grounds, but the grass there is altogether too well combed to be ruffled by unruly boys. If a boy's cousin comes in from the country, and he wishes to try conclusions with him, he must confine his efforts to the flagged sidewalk or the cobble-stoned street, while a brass-buttoned referee is likely at any moment to interfere, and take them both into custody for disorderly conduct.

Again, outside of a boy's ball-playing, scarce one of his other pastimes does much to build him up. Swimming is excellent, but is confined to a very few months in the year, and is seldom gone at, as it should be, with any regularity, or with a competent teacher to gradually lead the boy on to its higher possibilities. Skating is equally desultory, because in many of our cities winters pass with scarcely a week of good ice. Coasting brings some up-hill walking, good for the legs, but does practically nothing for the arms.

So boyhood slips along until the lad is well on in his teens, and still, in nine cases out of ten, he has had nothing yet of any account in the way of that systematic, vigorous, daily exercise which looks directly to his weak points, and aims not only to eradicate them, but to build up his general health and strength as well. He gets no help in the one place of all where he might so easily get it—the school. So far as we can learn, no system of exercise has been introduced into any school or college in this land, unless it is at the military academy at West Point, which begins to do for each pupil, not alone what might easily be done, but what actually *ought* to be done. It will probably not be many years before all of us will wonder why the proper steps in this direction have been put off so long. Calisthenics are here and there resorted to. In some schools a rubber strap has been introduced, the pupil taking one end of it in each hand, and working it in a few different directions, but in a mild sort of way. At Amherst College enough has been accomplished to tell favorably on the present health of the student, but not nearly enough to make him strong and vigorous all over, so as to build him up against ill health in the future. At another college certain exercises, excellent in their way, admirable for suppling the joints and improving the carriage, have for some time been practised. But this physical work does not go nearly far enough, nor is it aimed sufficiently at each pupil's peculiar weak spot. It also neither reaches all the students, nor is it practised but a small part of the year. In the great majority of our schools and colleges, little or no idea is given the pupil as to the good results he will derive from exercise. The teacher's own experience in physical development is often more limited than that of some of his scholars.

The evil does not end here. Take the son of the man of means and refinement, a boy who is having given him as liberal an education as money can buy and his parents' best judgment can select, one who spends a third or more of his life in fitting himself to get on successfully in the remainder of it. That boy certainly ought to come out ready for his life's work, with not only a thoroughly-trained mind and a strong moral nature, but with a well-developed, vigorous physique, and a knowledge of how to maintain it, so that he may make the most of all his advantages.

But how often does this happen? Stand by the gate as the senior class of almost any college in this country files out from its last examination before graduation, and look the men carefully over. Ask your physician to join you in the scrutiny. If, between you two, you can arrive at the conclusion that one-half, or even one-third of them, have that vitality and stamina which make it probable that they will live till seventy, it will be indeed most surprising. A few of these young men, the athletes, will be well-developed, better really than they need be. But this over-development may be far from the safest or wisest course. Even though physically improved by it, it is not certain that this marked development will carry them onward through life to a ripe old age. But, with others indifferently developed, there will be many more positively weak. Such men may have bright, uncommon heads. Yes; but a bright and uncommon head on a broken down, or nearly broken down, body is not going to make half as effective a man in the life-race as a little duller head and a good deal better body.

But have these graduates had a competent instructor at college to look after them in this respect? Will some one name a college where they have such an instructor? or a school where, instead of building the pupil up for the future, more has been done than to insure his present health? One or two such there may be, but scarcely more than one or two.

Take even the student who has devoted the most time to severe muscular exercise—the rowing-man, not the beginner, but the veteran of a score or more of races, who has been rowing all his four college years as regularly and almost as often as he dined. Certainly it will not be claimed that his is not a well-developed body, or that his permanent health is not insured. Let us look a little at him and see. What has he done? He entered college at eighteen, and is the son, say, of a journalist or of a professional man. Finding, when he came to be fourteen or fifteen, that he was not strong, that somehow he did not fill out his clothes, he put in daily an hour or more at the gymnasium, walked much at intervals, took sparring lessons, did some rowing, and perhaps, by the time he entered college, got his upper arm to be a foot or even thirteen inches in circumference, with considerable muscle on his chest. Now this young man hears daily, almost hourly, of the wonderful Freshman crew—an embryotic affair as yet, to be sure, but of exalted expectations—and into that crew he must go at all hazards. He is tried and accepted. Now, for four years, if a faithful oar, he will row all of a thousand miles a year. As each year has, off and on, not over two hundred rowing-days in all, he will generally, for the greater part of the remaining time, pull nearly an equivalent daily at the rowing-weights. He will find a lot of eager fellows at his side, working their utmost to outdo him, and get that place in the boat which he so earnestly covets, and which he is not yet quite sure that he can hold. Some of his muscles are developing fast. His recitations are, perhaps, suffering a little, but never mind that just now, when he thinks that there is more important work on hand. The young fellow's appetite is ravenous. He never felt so hearty in his life, and is often told how well he is looking. He attracts attention because likely to be a representative man. He never filled out his clothes as he does now. His legs are improving noticeably. They ought to do so, for it is not one or two miles, but three or four, which he runs on almost every one of those days in the hundred in which he is not rowing.

Our young athlete has not always gone into the work from mere choice. For instance, one of a recent Harvard Freshman crew told the writer that he had broken down his eyes from over-use of them, and, looking about for some vigorous physical exercise which would tone him up quickly and restore his eyesight, and having no one to consult, he had taken to rowing.

The years roll by till the whole four are over, and our student is about to graduate. He looks back to see what he has accomplished. In physical matters he finds that, while he is a skilful, and perhaps a decidedly successful, oar, and that some of his measurements have much improved since the day he was first measured, others somehow have not come up nearly as fast, in fact, have held back in the most surprising way. His chest-girth may be three or even four inches larger for the four years' work. Some, if not much, of that is certainly the result of growth, not development, and, save what running did, the rest is rather an increase of the back muscles than of front and back alike. Strong as his back is—for many a hard test has it stood in the long, hot home-minutes of more than one well-fought race—still he has not yet a thoroughly developed and capacious chest. Doubtless his legs have improved, if he has done any running. (In some colleges the rowing-men scarcely run at all.) His calves have come to be well-developed and shapely, and so too have his thighs, while his loins are noticeably strong-looking and well muscled up, and so indeed is his whole back. But if he has done practically no other arm-work than that which rowing and the preparation for it called for, his arms are not so large, especially above the elbow, as they ought to be for a man with such legs and such a back. The front of his chest is not nearly so well developed as his back, perhaps is hardly developed at all, and he is very likely to carry himself inerectly, with head and neck canted somewhat forward, while there is a lack of fulness, often a noticeable hollowness, of the upper chest, till the shoulders are plainly warped and rounded forward.

Fig. 1.

Fig. 2.

With professional oarsmen, who for years have rowed far more than they have done anything else, and who have no especial care for their looks, or spur to develop harmoniously, the defects rowing leaves stand out most glaringly. Notice in the cuts on pp. 36, 37 (Figs. 1 and 2) the flat and slab-sided, almost hollow, look about the upper chest and front shoulder, and compare these with the full and well-rounded make of the figure whose body is sketched on the cover. It will not take long to determine which has the better front chest, or which is likely to so carry that chest as to ward off tendencies to throat and lung troubles. Yet Fig. 1 is from a photograph of one of the most distinguished student-oarsmen America ever produced, while Fig. 2 represents one of the swiftest and most skilful professional scullers of the country to-day.[A] Better proof could not be presented of the effect of a great amount of rowing, and of the very limited exercise it brings to those muscles which are not especially called on.

After the student's rowing is over, and his college days are past, and he settles down to work with not nearly so much play in it, how does he find that his rowing pays? Has it made him fitter than his fellows, who went into athletics with no such zeal and devotion, to stand life's wear and tear, especially when that life is to be spent mainly in-doors? When, in later years, with new associations, business cares, and long, hard head-work, accompanied, as the latter usually is, by only partial inflation of the lungs, when all these get him out of the way of using his large back muscles, he will find their very size, and the long spell of warping forward which so much rowing gave the shoulders, tends more to weigh him forward than if he had never so developed them. Instead of benefiting his throat and lungs, this abnormal development actually inclines to cramp them.

Here, then, is the case of a man who voluntarily gave much time, thought, and labor to the severest test of his strength, and who had hoped to bring about staying powers, and he comes out of it all, to begin his real race in life, often no better fitted, perhaps not nearly so well fitted, for it as some of his comrades who did not spare half so much time to athletics. The other men, who did not work nearly as much as he did, still managed to hit upon a sort which, instead of cramping their chests, expanded them, enlarging the lung-room, and so gave the heart, stomach, and other vital organs all the freest play.

If the ordinary play and exercise of the boy do not build and round him into a sound, well-made, and evenly-balanced man; if the hardest work he has hit on, when left to himself to find out, mostly to be paid for by a considerable amount of money; if these only leave him a half-developed man, can it not be seen at once that an improvement is wanted in his physical education?

Are we not behindhand, and far behindhand, then, in a matter of serious importance to the well-being of the people of our country? Do we not want some system of education which shall rear men, not morally and intellectually good alone, but good physically as well? which shall qualify them both to seize and to make the most of the advantages which years of toil and struggle bring, but which advantages among us now are too frequently thrown away. Men too often, just as they are about clutching these benefits, find, Tantalus-like, that they are eluding their grasp. The reason must be plain to all. It is because that grasp is weakening, and falls powerless at the very time when it could be and should be surest, and potent for the most good.

CHAPTER III.

WILL DAILY PHYSICAL EXERCISE FOR GIRLS PAY?

OBSERVE the girls in any of our cities or towns, as they pass to or from school, and see how few of them are at once blooming, shapely, and strong. Some are one or the other, but very few are all combined, while a decided majority are neither one of them. Instead of high chests, plump arms; comely figures, and a graceful and handsome mien, you constantly see flat chests, angular shoulders, often round and warped forward, with scrawny necks, pipe-stem arms, narrow backs, and a weak walk. Not one girl in a dozen is thoroughly erect, whether walking, standing, or sitting. Nearly every head is pitched somewhat forward. The arms are frequently held almost motionless, and there is a general lack of spring and elasticity in their movements. Fresh, blooming complexions are so rare as to attract attention. Among eyes, plenty of them pretty, sparkling, or intelligent, but few have vigor and force. If any dozen girls, taken at random, should place their hands side by side on a table, many, if not most, of these hands would be found to lack beauty and symmetry, the fingers, and indeed the whole hand, too often having a weak, undeveloped, nerveless look.

Now watch these girls at play. See how few of their games bring them really vigorous exercise. Set them to running, and hardly one in the party has the swift, graceful, gliding motion she might so readily acquire. Not one can run any respectable distance at a good pace. There is abundant vivacity and spirit, abundant willingness to play with great freedom, but very little such play as there might be, and which would pay so well. Most of their exercise worth calling vigorous is for their feet alone, the hands seldom having much to do. The girls of the most favored classes are generally the poorest players. The quality and color of their clothing necessitates their avoiding all active, hearty play, while it is the constant effort of nurse or governess to repress that superabundance of spirits which ought to belong to every boy and girl. Holding one's elbows close to the body while walking, and keeping the hands nearly or quite motionless, may accord with the requirements of fashionable life, but it's terribly bad for the arms, keeping them poor, indifferent specimens, when they might be models of grace and beauty.

As the girl comes home from school, not with one book only, but often six or eight, instead of looking light and strong and free, she is too often what she really appears to be, pale and weak. So many books suggest a large amount of work for one day, certainly for one evening, and the impression received is that she is overworked, while the truth frequently is that the advance to be made in each book is but trifling, and the aggregate, not at all large, by no means too great for the same girl were she strong and hearty. It is not the mental work which is breaking her down, but there is no adequate physical exercise to build her up. See what ex-Surgeon-General Hammond says, in his work on "Sleep", as to the ability to endure protracted brain-work without ill result:

"It is not the mere quantity of brain-work which is the chief factor in the production of disease. The emotional conditions under which work is performed is a far more important matter. A man of trained mental habits can bear with safety an almost incredible amount of brain-toil, provided he is permitted to work without distraction or excitement, in the absence of disquieting cares and anxieties. It is not brain-work, in fact, that kills, but brain-*worry*."

The girl, of course, has not the strength for the protracted effort of the matured man, nor is such effort often required of her. Her studying is done quietly at home, undisturbed, usually, by any such cares and responsibilities as the man encounters. Hers is generally brain-work, not brain-worry. Yet the few hours a day exhaust her, because her vital system, which supports her brain, is feeble and inefficient. No girl is at school over six hours out of the twenty-four, and, deducting the time taken for recitation, recess, and the various other things which are not study, five hours, or even less, will cover the time she gives to actual brain-work in school, with two, or perhaps three, hours daily out of school. With the other sixteen hours practically her own, there is ample time for all the vigorous physical exercise she needs or could take, and yet allow ten, or even twelve, of those hours for sleep or eating. But notice, in any of these off-hours, what exercise these girls take. They walk to and fro from school, they play a few minutes at recess, they may take an occasional irregular stroll besides, and may indulge in a game of croquet, but all the time intent on their conversation, never thinking of the exercise itself, and the benefit it brings. Such things fill up the measure of the daily physical exercise of thousands of our American girls. It is the same thing for nearly all, save those from the poorest classes.

And what is the result? Exactly what such exercise—or, rather, such lack of it—would bring. The short, abrupt run, the walk to or from school, the afternoon stroll, or the miscellaneous standing about—none of these call for or beget strength of limb, depth of chest, or vitality. None of these exercises is more than almost any flat-chested, half-developed girl could readily accomplish without serious effort, and, going through them for years, she would need little more strength than she had at first.

But all this time her mental work comes in no meagre allowance. *It* is all the time pushing forward. Subjects are set before her, to grasp and master which requires every day hours of close application for months together. The number of them is also enlarging, and the task is constantly becoming more severe. A variety of influences spurs her steadily onward. Maybe it is emulation and determination which urges her on, not only to do well, but to excel. Maybe it is to gratify the teacher's pride, and a desire to show the good fruit of her work. Perhaps oftener than anything else the girl is in dread of being dropped into another class, and she resolves to remain with her present one at all hazards.

But with all this there is an advance in the amount and difficulty of the brain-work. No distinction is made between the delicate girl and the strong one. To those of a like age come like tasks. The delicate girl, from her indifference to physical effort, finding that for the time her weakness of body does not interfere with a ready-working brain, gradually inclines to draw even more away from livelier games and exercises, in which she does not excel, and to get more at her books. Can there be much doubt as to the result a few years later? Is it any wonder that the neglected body develops some partial weakness, or too often general debility? Is it at all a rare thing, in the observation of any one, to notice that this weakness, this debility, are very apt to become chronic, and that the woman, later on in life, is a source of anxiety and a burden to her friends, when instead of this she might have been a valued helper?

Now, if the body, during the growing years, was called on to do nothing which should even half develop it, while the brain was pushed nearly to its utmost, does it take long to decide whether such a course was a wise one? Leaving out entirely the discomfort to the body, is that a sensible system of education which leaves a girl liable to become weak, if not entirely broken down, before she is well on in middle age? Is this not like giving great care to moral and mental education alone, and actually doing almost nothing for their physical nature? Is this not an irrational and one-sided course, and sure to beget a one-sided person? And yet is not that just what is going on to-day with a great majority of the young girls in our land?

The moment it is conceded that a delicate body can be made a robust one, that moment it is equally plain that there can be an almost incalculable gain in the comfort and usefulness of the possessor of that body, not only during all the last half of her life, but through the first half as well. And yet, to persons familiar with what judicious, daily physical exercise has done, and can do, for a delicate body, there is no more doubt but that this later strength, and even sturdiness, can be acquired than that the algebra or geometry, which at first seems impenetrable, can be gradually mastered. The rules which bring success in each are in many respects identical. Begin to give the muscles of the hand and forearm, for instance, as vigorous and assiduous use as these mathematical studies bring to the brain, and the physical grasp will as surely and steadily improve as does the mental. Give not only the delicate girls, but all girls, exercises which shall insure strong and shapely limbs, and chests deep, full, and high, beginning these exercises mildly, and progressing very gradually, correcting this high shoulder, or that stoop, or this hollow chest, or that overstep, and carrying on this development as long as the school-days last. Let this be done under a teacher as familiar with her work as the mathematical instructor is with his, and what incalculable benefit would accrue, not to this generation alone, but to their descendants as well!

But will not this physical training dull the mind for its work? If protracted several hours, or the greater part of each day, as with the German peasant-woman in the field, or the Scotch fish-woman with her wares, no doubt it would. But if Maclaren of Oxford wanted but a little while each day to increase the girth of the chests of a dozen British soldiers three inches apiece in four months, is this very moderate allowance likely to work much mental dulness? Did Charles Dickens's seven to twelve miles afoot daily interfere with some masterly work which his pen produced each day? Did Napoleon's whole days spent in the saddle tell very seriously on his mental operations, and prevent him from conceiving and carrying out military and strategic work which will compare favorably with any the world's history tells of?

And what if this daily exercise, beside the bodily benefit and improvement which ensues, should also bring actually better mental work? Unbending the bow for a little while, taking the tension from the brain for a few minutes, and depleting it by expanding the chest to its fullest capacity, and increasing the circulation in the limbs—these, instead of impairing that brain, will repair it, and markedly improve its tone and vigor.

There ought to be in every girls' school in our land, for pupils of every age, a system of physical culture which should first eradicate special weaknesses and defects, and then create and maintain the symmetry of the pupils, increasing their bodily vigor and strength up to maturity. If several, or a majority, of the girls in a class have flat or indifferent chests, put them in a squad which shall pay direct and steady attention to raising, expanding, and strengthening the chest. If many have a bad gait, some stepping too long, others too short, set them aside for daily special attention to their step. If many, or nearly all, have an inerect carriage, wholly lacking *la ligne* of Dumas, then daily insist on such exercises for them as shall straighten them up and keep them up. The dancing-master teaches the girl to step gracefully and accurately through various dancing-steps. To inculcate a correct length of step, and method of putting the foot down and raising it in walking, is not nearly so difficult a task. If the "setting-up" drill of the West Pointer in a few weeks transforms the raw and ungainly country boy into a youth of erect and military bearing, and insisting on that bearing at all times throughout the first year gives the cadet a set and carriage which he often retains through life, is there anything to hinder the girl from acquiring an equally erect and handsome carriage of the body if she too will only use the means? If the muscles which, when fully developed, enable one to sit or stand erect for hours together are now weak, is it not wise to at once strengthen them?

But may not this vigorous muscular exercise, which tends to produce hard and knotted muscles in the man, take away the softer and more graceful lines, which are essentially feminine? If exercise be kept up for hours together, as in the case of the blacksmith, undoubtedly it would. But that is a thing a sensible system of exercise would avoid, as studiously as it would the weakness and inefficiency which result from no work. A little trial soon tells what amount of work, and how much of it, is best adapted to each pupil; then the daily maintaining of that proportion or kind of exercise, and its increase, as the newly-acquired strength justifies and invites it, is all that is required. Without that hardness and solidity which are essentially masculine, there still comes a firmness and plumpness of muscle to which the unused arm or back was a stranger. Instead of these being incompatible with beauty, they are directly accessory to it. "Elegance of form in the human figure," says Emerson, "marks some excellence of structure;" and again, "any real increase of fitness to its end, in any fabric or organism, is an increase of beauty."

Look at the famous beauties of any age, and everything in the picture or statue points to this same firmness and symmetry of make, this freedom from either leanness or flabbiness. The Venuses and Junos, the Minervas, Niobes, and Helens of mythology, the Madonnas, the mediæval beauties, all alike have the well-developed and shapely arm and shoulder, the high chest, the vigorous body, and the firm and erect carriage. Were there a thin chest or a flat shoulder, a poor and feeble arm or a contracted waist, it would at once mar the picture, and bring down on it judgment anything but favorable. Put now on the canvas or in marble, not the strongest and most comely, neither the weakest and least-favored, of our American girls or women, but simply her who fairly represents the average, and, however well the face and expression might suffice, the imperfect physical development, and indifferent figure and carriage, would at once justly provoke unfavorable comment.

That the same vigorous exercise and training which brought forth womanly physical beauty in ancient days will bring it out now, there need be no manner of doubt. A most apt and excellent case in point was mentioned in the *New York Tribune* of June 19th, 1878. It said:

"The study and practice of gymnastics are to be made compulsory in all the State schools in Italy. The apostle of physical culture in that enervating climate is Sebastian Fenzi, the son of a Florence banker. He built a gymnasium at his own expense in that city, and from that beginning the movement has extended from city to city. He has preached gymnastics to senators and deputies, to the syndic and municipal councillors, and even to the crown princess, now queen. *He especially inculcates its advantages on all mothers of families, as likely to increase to a remarkable extent the personal charms of their daughters.* And so far as his own domestic experience goes, his theories have not been contradicted by practice, for *he is the father of the most beautiful women in Italy.*"

Suppose Mr. Durant at Wellesley, or Mr. Caldwell at Vassar, should at once introduce in their deservedly famous schools a system of physical education which should proceed on the simple but intelligent plan, first of training the weaker muscles of each pupil until they are as strong as the rest, and then of transferring the young woman thus physically improved from the class of this or that special work, to that which insures to all muscles alike ample, daily vigorous exercise. Suppose that all the girls could be made to consider this daily lesson as much a matter of course in their studies as anything else. Suppose, again, that there is a teacher familiar with the work and all its requirements, one who is capable of interesting others, one who fully enters into the spirit of it. If such a master or mistress can be found, if the pupils are instructed—whether they be sitting, standing, or walking—to always remain erect, is there any reason why the Vassar girls should not soon have as fine and impressive a carriage as the manly young fellows at the academy across the river, but a few miles distant?

Looking again at the effect on the mental work, would the daily half-hour of exercise in-doors, and the hour's constitutional out-doors, in all weathers, if sensibly arranged, interfere one whit with all the intellectual progress the girls could or should make? For, is that a rational system of intellectual progress which brings out a bright intellect on a half-developed body, and promises fine things in the future, when the body has had no training adequate to justify the belief that there will be much of any future? Is not that rather a dear price to pay for such intellectuality? Hear Herbert Spencer on this point:

"On women the effects of this forcing system are, if possible, even more injurious than on men. Being in a great measure debarred from those vigorous and enjoyable exercises of body by which boys mitigate the evils of excessive study, girls feel these evils in their full intensity. Hence the much smaller proportion of them who grow up well-made and healthy. In the pale, angular, flat-chested young ladies, so abundant in London drawing-rooms, we see the effect of merciless application unrelieved by youthful sports; and this physical degeneracy exhibited by them hinders their welfare far more than their many accomplishments aid it. Mammas anxious to make their daughters attractive could scarcely choose a course more fatal than this which sacrifices the body to the mind. Either they disregard the tastes of the opposite sex, or else their conception of those tastes is erroneous. Men care comparatively little for erudition in women, but very much for physical beauty and good nature and sound sense. How many conquests does the blue-stocking make through her extensive knowledge of history?"

This is a question quite worthy of the consideration of every teacher of girls in our land, and a paragraph full of suggestion, not only to every parent having a child's interests in his or her keeping, but to every spirited girl herself as well.

Every school-girl in America could be daily practised in a few simple exercises, calling for no costly, intricate, or dangerous apparatus, taking a little time, but yet expanding her lungs, invigorating her circulation, strengthening her digestion, giving every muscle and joint of her body vigorous play, and so keeping her toned up, and strong enough to be free from much danger either of incurring serious disease, or any of the lighter ailments so common among us. As to her usefulness, no matter where her lot is to be cast, it will be increased, and, it is not too much to add, her happiness would be greatly enhanced through all her life as well.

CHAPTER IV.

IS IT TOO LATE FOR WOMEN TO BEGIN?

But if the school-days are past and the girl has become a woman, what then? If the girl, trammelled by few duties outside of school-hours, has found amusement for herself, yet still needs daily and regular exercise to make and keep her fresh and hearty, much more does the woman, especially in a country like our own, where physical exercise for her sex is almost unknown, require such exercise. Our women are born of parents who pride themselves on their mental qualifications, on a good degree of intelligence. Our educational system is one which offers an endless variety of spurs to continued mental effort.

Are not the majority of our women to-day, especially in town and city, physically weak? The writers on nervous disorders speak of the astounding increase of such diseases among us, of late years, in both sexes, but especially among the women. General debility is heard of nowadays almost as often as General Grant. Most of our women think two miles, or even less, a long distance to walk, even at a dawdling pace, while few of them have really strong chests, backs, or arms. (If they wish to test their arms, for instance, let them grasp a bar or the rung of a ladder, and try to pull themselves up once till the chin touches. Not two in fifty will do it, but almost any boy can.) Hardly a day goes by when a woman's strength is not considerably taxed, and often overtaxed.

There is no calling of the unmarried woman where vigorous health and strength—not great or herculean, but simply such as every well-built and well-developed woman ought to have—would not be of great, almost priceless value to her. The shop-girl, the factory operative, the clerk in the store, the book-keeper, the seamstress, the milliner, the telegraph operator, are all confined, for many hours a day, with exercise for but a few of the muscles, and with the trunk held altogether too long in one position, and that too often a contracted and unhealthy one. Actually nothing is done to render the body lithe and supple, to develop the idle muscles, to deepen the breathing and quicken the circulation—in short, to tone up the whole system. No wonder such a day's work, and such a way of living, leaves the body tired and exhausted. It would, before long, do the same for the strongest man. No wonder that the walk to and from work is a listless affair. No wonder that, later on, special or general weakness develops, and the woman goes through life either weak and delicate, or with not half the strength and vigor which might readily be hers.

And is it any better with the married woman? Take one of limited means. Much of the work about her home which servants might do, could she employ them, she bravely does herself, willing to make ten times this sacrifice, if need be, for those dearest to her. Follow her throughout the day, especially where there are children: there is an almost endless round of duties, many of them not laborious, to be sure, or calling for much muscular strength, but keeping the mind under a strain until they are done, difficult to encompass because difficult to foresee. In the aggregate they are almost numberless. A man can usually tell in the morning most of what is in front of him for the day —indeed, can often plan so as to say beforehand just what he will be at each hour. But not so the housewife and mother of young children. She is constantly called to perform little duties, both expected and unexpected, which cannot fail to tell on a person not strong. A healthy child a year old will often weigh twenty pounds; yet a woman otherwise weak will carry that child on her left arm several times a day up one or more flights of stairs, till you would think she would drop from exhaustion. Let sickness come, and she will often seem almost tireless, so devotedly will she keep the child in her arms. While children are, of course, carried less when they begin to walk, many a child two, or even three years old, is picked up by the mother, not a few times a day, even though he weighs thirty or forty pounds instead of twenty. Now for this mother to have handled a dumb-bell of that weight would have been thought foolish and dangerous, for nothing about her suggested strength equal to that performance. And yet the devotion of a weak mother to her child is quite as great as that of a strong one. Is it any wonder that this overdoing of muscles never trained to such work must sooner or later tell? It would be wonderful if it did not.

Yet now, suppose that same mother had from early childhood been trained to systematic physical exercise suited to her strength, and increasing with that strength until, from a strong and healthy child, she grew to be a hearty, vigorous woman, well developed, strong, and comely—what now would she mind carrying the little tot on her arm? What before soon became heavy and a burden—a willing burden though it was—now never seems so at all, and really is no task for such muscles as she now has. Instead of her day's work breaking her down, it is no more than a woman of her vigor needs—indeed, not so much as she needs—to keep her well and strong.

And, besides escaping the bodily tire and exhaustion, look at the happiness it brings her in the exhilaration which comes with ruddy health, in the feeling of being easily equal to whatever comes up, in being a stranger to indigestion, to nervousness and all its kindred ailments. This vital force, sparing her many of the doubts and fears so common to the weak, but which the strong seldom know, enables her to endure patiently privation, watching, and bereavement. And who is the more likely to live to a ripe old age, the woman who never took suitable and adequate exercise to give her even moderate vitality and strength, or she who, by a judicious and sensible system, suited to her particular needs, has developed such powers?

But, while this is all well enough for young girls, is it not too late for full-grown women to attempt to get the same benefits? The girl was young and plastic, and, with proper care, could be moulded in almost any way; but the woman already has her make and set, and these cannot readily be changed. Perhaps not quite so readily, but actual trial will show that the difficulty is largely imaginary. To many, indeed to most women, the idea is absolutely new, and they never supposed such change possible. Bryant, beginning at forty, made exercise pay wonderfully. Bear in mind how, with a few minutes a day, Maclaren enlarged and strengthened men thirty years old; that, out of his class of over a hundred, the greatest gain was in the oldest man in it, and he was thirty-five. Let us look at what one or two women have managed to effect by systematic and thorough bodily training. In "The Coming Man" Charles Reade says (p. 50), "Nathalie, a French gymnast, and not a woman of extraordinary build, can take two fifty-six-pound weights from the ground, one in each hand, and put them slowly above her head." She has "a sister who goes up the slack-rope. Farini saw her pitted against twenty sailors. The sailors had a slack-rope; she had another. A sailor went up as far as he could; the gymnast went as high on her rope at the same time. Sailor came down tired, the lady fresh. Another sailor went up, the lady ditto; and so on. *She wore out the whole twenty, having gone up an aggregate of feet higher than St. Peter's Church at Rome.* This feat is due to great strength, complete either-handedness, and the athlete's power of pinching a rope with the sinews of the lower limbs."

But is this great and unusual strength, especially of the arms, desirable in most women? Not at all; but that is not the point. When Farini says that the first step toward making one a skilled gymnast or acrobat is to bring up the weak arm, and shoulder, and side—usually the left—until equally strong with its, till now, superior mate, and that he is constantly doing that, he is doing more by far than would be needed to make most women, not as strong as acrobats and performers, but—a far more important matter—reasonably and comfortably so, sufficiently to keep nervous disorders away, to enable them to be far better equal to the daily duties, and to spend life with an appreciation and zest too often unknown by the weak woman; finally, to preserve for a woman the bloom and healthy look which once in a while she sees, even in a woman of advanced years, and which would be her own did she use the means to have it.

And what should a woman do to get this health and strength and bloom? Just what is done by the young girl. Indeed, there are a hundred exercises, almost any of which, faithfully followed up, would help directly to bring the desired result. With her, as with girl or man or boy, the first thing is to symmetrize, to bring up the weaker muscles by special effort, calling them at once into vigorous action, and to restore to its proper position the shoulder, back, or chest, which has been so long allowed to remain out of place. The symmetry once gained, then equal work for all the muscles, taken daily, and in such quantities as are found to suit best.

The variety of exercises open to woman, especially out-of-doors, is almost as great as to man. Every one knows some graceful horsewoman, and it is a pity there were not a hundred where there is one. One of the most expert of our acquaintance is the mother of one of the most gifted metaphysicians in the land, and he already is a middle-aged man. There are a few ladies in this country, and a good many in England, who think nothing of a five or six mile walk daily, and an occasional one of twice that length. Once in a while a married woman here will do some long-distance skating. In Holland, in the season, it is with many an every-day affair. Some of the best swimmers and floaters at the watering-places are women, and they certainly do not look much troubled with nervousness. More than one woman has distinguished herself in Alpine climbing. The writer once saw a woman, apparently about twenty-eight, a handsome, vigorous, rosy Englishwoman, row her father from Putney to Mortlake, on the Thames, a distance of four miles and three furlongs, not at racing pace, to be sure, but at a lively speed. The measured precision of that lady's stroke, the stately poise of the body and head, and the clean, neat, and effective feathering, would have done credit to an old Oxford oar.

What woman has done, woman may do. Bind one arm in a sling, and keep it utterly idle for a month, and meanwhile ply the other busily with heavy work, such as swinging a hammer, axe, or dumb-bell, and is it hard to say which will be the healthier, the plumper, the stronger—the *live* arm, at the end of the month? And will this only apply to men's arms, and not to women's? Who has usually the stronger, and almost generally the shapelier arm—the woman who, surrounded with servants, takes her royal ease, and has American notions and ways of exercise, or the busy maid in her kitchen? If the latter's arm is large, yet not well-proportioned, it simply means that some of its muscles have been used far more than the others.

Now, to her who understands what exercises will develop each of the

29

muscles of that arm, and who can tell at sight which are fully developed or developed at all, and which are not, it is easy to bring up the backward ones, and so secure the symmetry and the consequent general strength. The same rule holds good of all the other muscles, as well as those of the arm.

Plenty of active out-door work will go far toward securing health. But it will only develop the parts brought into play, and there ought to be exercise for all.

Now what daily work, and how much of it, will secure this symmetry, erectness, and strength, supposing that, at the outset, there is no organic defect, but that the woman is simply weak both in her muscular and in her vital systems? In the first place, let it be understood that the connection between these systems is intimate, and that the judicious building and strengthening of the former, and the keeping up that strength by sensible daily exercise, tells directly on the latter. Vigorous muscular exercise, properly taken, enlarges the respiration, quickens the circulation, improves the digestion, the working, in fact, of all the vital parts. Dr. Mitchell says it is the very thing also to quiet the excited nerves and brain.

The amount of that exercise daily depends on the present strength of the woman. If she is weak generally, for the first fortnight the exercise, while general enough to bring all the muscles into play, must be light and easy. Then, as a little strength is gained, the work advances accordingly. If partially strong at first, invariably the first thing to do is to adapt the exercise mainly to the weaker muscles till they catch up.

Suppose the right arm is stronger than the left, as frequently happens, because it has had more to do. For the first month—or, if necessary, for the first two months—let the left arm have nearly all the exercise, and that exercise as vigorous as it can comfortably take. Then, when it is found that it can lift or carry as heavy a weight, and pull or push as hard as the right, keep at it, by means of exercise, until both arms can do the same amount of work, and are equal. But suppose the arms are already equally strong, or, rather, equally weak—that both the back and chest are small; that is, not so large or well-proportioned as they should be in a well-built woman of a certain height —then all that is necessary is to select work especially adapted to strengthen the back, and other work telling directly on the chest. For the first fortnight very mild efforts should be made, and the advance should be gradual, taking great care never once to overdo it. Let the advance be made as the newly-acquired strength justifies and encourages it. What particular exercises will effect the strengthening and development of any given muscles will be pointed out in the chapter on Special Exercise, at the latter part of this book.

How about the length of time this daily exercising will take? It is all easy enough for the rich, whose time is their own, and who could spare four or five hours a day if necessary; but how is the woman to manage it who must work from seven to six, or even far into the evening as well? She can hardly get time to read about horseback riding and Alpine climbing, much less take part in them. Well, it is a poor system which cannot suit nearly all cases. The woman who works steadily from early morning till well into the night, especially at employment at all sedentary and confining, is undergoing a test and a hardship which will certainly call for a strong constitution, good condition, and a brave spirit as well, or the strain will surely break her down, and bring to her permanent weakness. If so many hours must be spent in labor, then let her secure ten or fifteen minutes, upon rising, for a series of exercises in her room. At the dinner-hour, again at supper-time, and once about mid-morning, and again at mid-afternoon, three or five minutes could generally be spared for a few brisk exercises calculated to limber and call into vigorous action the back, and many of the muscles so long held almost motionless until they stiffen from it. If there is a whole hour at dinner-time, and half of it could be spent in walking, if possible with a cheerful and energetic companion, who would make her forget the dull routine of her day —not dawdling, aimless walking, but stepping out as if she meant it, with a spring and energy which quickens the pulse, driving the morning's thoughts out of the mind, scattering low spirits to the winds—it would bring a pleasant feeling of recreation and change. The benefit to be derived from such a walk would be immediate and marked.

Is this asking much? A mile and a half could easily be covered in that time, and, by a strong walker, even two, while the dinner would taste twice as good for the exercise. Another mile, or even half a mile, might be walked at supper-time, the pace always being kept up. If the confinement is so close as not to permit even these few snatches of time for a little recreation, never mind. Do not give it up yet. The ten minutes on rising were made sure of anyhow.[B] Yes, another chance remains. When at last the work is over, even though it is time to retire, get out-of-doors for half an hour's smart walk with brother or friend, and see how refreshing it will prove. The jaded body will almost forget its tire, and the sleep which follows, while it may not be quite as long as before, will make up in quality, and the new day will find a far fresher woman, one better up to her duties, than if no exercise had been taken.

To her who does not labor so long, but has her evenings to herself, unless already broken by disease, there need be no trouble about getting strong and healthy. Let her do the little exercise above mentioned till evening; then, first eating a hearty supper, beginning with such distance as she can walk easily, add to the distance gradually, until she finds herself equal to four or five miles at a smart pace for her—say three and a half miles to the hour. (The professional masculine pedestrians do eight miles an hour, to be sure; but Miss Von Hillern, for instance, is good for about six.) This, taken either every evening, or, say, four evenings a week, will soon give tone, and make the woman feel strong instead of weak, will enable her to digest what she eats, and will visibly improve her appetite. Let her give five or ten minutes for exercising the arms and chest before retiring, and she has had abundant exercise for that day, while any trouble she has had in the past about sleeping is at an end.

But sufficient as the evening walk is, of course if it can be had in daylight and in the sunshine, it is all the better. Few mothers are so placed that they cannot each day, by good management, get an hour for the care of their health. Let them be sure to take a quick, lively walk for the whole time, not with arms held motionless, but swinging easily as men's do—of course, for the first month taking less distances, but working steadily on. They will be astonished at the very gratifying difference in the result between it and the old listless walk, and how much easier the day's duties come now.

But there is one class of women who are especially favored—a large class too, in our land—the daughters of parents so well to do that, between their graduation from school and the day they are married, their time is practically their own. If weak at the start, let them, after gradual exercise begins to make them stronger, take more besides the few minutes at rising and retiring, and the hearty constitutional afoot. If their walking is done in the afternoon, let them set apart half an hour in the latter part of the morning (if possible, with another girl similarly placed) for work which shall strengthen the arms and the whole trunk. If there is a good gymnasium convenient—especially if it has a teacher of the right stamp—there will be the best place for this work. But if not, a little home gymnasium like that suggested later in the chapter on that subject, and which every girl ought to have, would be the place. Very soon this extra work will tell. Look what the four hours a week, just with two-pound wooden dumb-bells, very light Indian clubs, and light pulley-weights, did for a youth of nineteen in one year![C] An increase of an inch in height, of one and a half around the upper arm, of three and a half inches in the girth of the chest, of fifteen pounds in weight—would not these work marked changes in any young woman, and would they not nearly always be most desirable changes? It is not a matter of inches and pounds alone. This increase of girth and weight is almost sure to tell most beneficially on the health and spirits as well—in short, on the general vigor.

If, with the increase in size and strength, care has been taken to practise special exercises to make and keep her erect, to at all times, whether sitting, standing, or walking, hold the head and neck where they should be, there is not much doubt but that, even in one short year, the difference in any girl, not strong or straight at the beginning, will be very marked. It really lies with young women of this class to make themselves physically—in proportion to their height—what they will.

Is there any need of pointing out to a spirited girl the value of a sound, healthy, and shapely body? Is there any sphere in woman's life where it will not stand her in good stead, and render her far more efficient at whatever she is called on to do—as daughter, sister, wife or mother, teacher or friend? Nor is the benefit limited even to her own lifetime, but her posterity are blessed by it as well. Would she like to have inherited consumptive tendencies, for instance, from her parent? Will her children like any better to inherit the same from her? In our Christian lands, we find, if history be correct, that the great men have almost invariably had remarkable mothers, while their fathers were as often nothing unusual. The Sandwich Island proverb, "If strong be the frame of the mother, her sons will make laws for the people," suggests truths that will hold good in many other places besides the Sandwich Islands. Let every intelligent girl and woman in this land bear in mind that, from every point of view, a vigorous and healthy body, kept toned up by rational, systematic, daily exercise, is one of the very greatest blessings which can be had in this world; that many persons spend tens of thousands of dollars in trying to regain even a part of this blessing when once they have lost it; that the means of getting it are easily within the reach of all, who are not already broken by disease; that it is never too late to begin, and that one hour a day, properly spent, is all that is needed to secure it.

CHAPTER V.
WHY MEN SHOULD EXERCISE DAILY.

T HE advantages to men of a well-built body, kept in thorough repair, are very great. Those of every class, whose occupation is sedentary, soon come to appreciate this. Some part of the machinery gets out of order. It may be the head, or eyes, or throat; it may be the lungs or stomach, liver or kidneys. Something does not go right. There is a clogging, a lack of complete action, and often positive pain. This physical clogging tells at once on the mental work, either making its accomplishment uncomfortable and an effort, or becoming so bad as to actually prevent work at all. It may make the man ill. There is very little doubt but that a large majority of ailments would be removed, or, rather, would never have come at all, had the lungs and also the muscles of the man had vigorous daily action to the extent that frequent trial had shown best suited to that man's wants. One of the quickest known ways of dispelling a headache is to give some of the muscles, those of the legs, for instance, a little hard, sharp work to do. The reason is obvious. Dr. Mitchell puts it well when he says that muscular exercise flushes the parts engaged in it, and so depletes the brain.

But fortunately that same exercise also helps make better blood, gets the entire lungs into action, quickens the activity of the other vital organs, and so tones up the whole man, that, if the exercise is taken daily and is kept up, disorder, unless very deep-seated, disappears.

It is well known that when the system, from any cause, gets run down, disease is more likely to enter, and slower at being shaken off. Thousands and hundreds of thousands of men and women have hard work, mental strain, fret and anxiety, daily, and for years together—indeed, scarcely do anything to lighten the tension in this direction. They tell you they are subject to headache or dyspepsia, or other disorder, as if it was out of the question to think of preventing it. But had the work been so arranged, as it nearly always could be —far oftener than most persons think—to secure daily an hour for vigorous muscular exercise for all the parts, this running down would, in most instances, never come. The sharp, hot work, till the muscles are healthily tired, insures the good digestion, the cleared brain, the sound sleep, the buoyant spirits.

The president of one of the largest banks in this country told the writer that, disappointed one summer in not getting a run to Europe, reflection told him that one marked benefit such jaunts had brought him was from the increased sleep he was enabled to get, that thereupon he determined on longer sleeps at home. He got them, and found, as he well put it, that he could "fight better." Beset all day long with men wanting heavy loans, that fighting tone, that ability to say "no" at the right time and in a way which showed he meant it, must have not only added to his own well-being, but to the bank's protection as well.

Again, many men are liable to occasionally have sudden and very protracted spells of head-work, where sleep and almost everything else must give way, so that the business in hand may be gotten through with. "Tom Brown" told the writer that, when in Parliament, he could work through a whole week together on but four hours of sleep a night, and be none the worse for it, provided he could have all he wanted the next week, and that since he was twenty-five he had hardly known a sick day.

A father, tired from his day of busy toil, may have a sick child, who for much of the night will not let him sleep. Such taxes as this, coming to one already run down and weak, cannot be braved frequently with impunity. Unless the five or six miles a day of Tom Brown and his fellow-Englishmen's "constitutional," or some equivalent, is resorted to, and the man kept well toned-up, one of these sudden calls may prove too severe, and do serious if not fatal injury. This toning-up is not all. If the bodily exercise is such as to get all the muscles strong, and keep them so, the very work that would otherwise overdo and exhaust now has no such effect, but is gone through with spirit and ease. There is that consciousness of strength which is equal to all such trifles.

The very nervousness and worry which used to be so wearing, at the sudden and ceaseless calls of the day, have gone, and for the reason that strong nerves and strong muscles are very liable to go together, and not to mind these things. What does the athlete at the top of his condition know about nervousness? He is blithe as a lark all the day long.

Dr. Mitchell says: "The man who lives an out-door life—who sleeps with the stars visible above him, who wins his bodily subsistence at first-hand from the earth and waters—is a being who defies rain and sun, has a strange sense of elastic strength, may drink if he likes, and may smoke all day long, and feel none the worse for it. Some such return to the earth for the means of life is what gives vigor and developing power to the colonists of an older race cast on a land like ours. A few generations of men living in such fashion store up a capital of vitality which accounts largely for the prodigal activity displayed by their descendants, and made possible only by the sturdy contest with nature which their ancestors have waged. That such a life is still led by multitudes of our countrymen is what alone serves to keep up our pristine force and energy."

Now, while this extreme hardiness and tone cannot be had by a person who has twelve hours of busy brain-work daily in-doors, and only one of bodily exercise, still, much can be done, quite enough to calm and tranquillize, and to carry easily over those passes which used to be dreaded.

If the man who habitually works too long without a rest would every hour or so turn lightly from his work, for even sixty seconds, to some vigorous exercise right in his office, or even in the next room or hall-way, until the blood got out of his brain a little, and the muscles tingled with a hearty glow, he would go back so refreshed as to quickly make up, both in the quantity and quality of his work, for the time lost. When his hour for exercise came, instead of having no heart for it, he would spring to it with alacrity, like the school-boy does to his play.

Even if the strong man does occasionally become jaded, he knows, as Hughes did, how to get back his strength and snap, and that a tired man is many removes from a tired-out one. There is a great deal in knowing whether your work is overdoing you or simply tiring you. One of the strongest and best oarsmen Harvard ever had, used, at first, to think he ought to stop rowing when he began to perspire, and was quite astounded when an older man told him that that was only the beginning of the real work. There is no end of comfort to a tired man, either mentally or physically, in the thought that sure relief is near.

Again, this relief by physical exercise will encourage the man to hope that, if war or accident do not cut him down, he may look for a long life, no matter how great may be the occasional strain. Few men, for instance, familiar with the life of the Duke of Wellington will claim that they are better workers than he was, or that they get through more in a day or year, or that, heavy as their responsibilities may be, they surpass or even equal those which were his for years together. Yet all the terrible mental strain this illustrious man underwent, battling with one of the greatest captains this world ever saw, all the exposure and forced marching, privation and toil, which come to the faithful soldier, and to him who holds the lives of multitudes in his hands, this man knew, and yet so controlled his work, exacting as it all was, as to manage to keep his body superior to all it was called on to do, and his mind in constant working order, and this not merely up to threescore and ten, but to fourscore good years, and three more besides. Did not the vigorous body at the start, and the daily attention to it, pay him?

Will it be claimed that the president of one of the best-known corporations on this continent did any more work than Wellington? That president was at it all day, and far into the night, and when away in Europe, nominally on a play-spell, as well. Naturally, he was a strong, energetic man; but he had so worked, and so neglected his body, that he died at fifty-two. Which of the two men showed the better sense?

What does cutting one's self down at fifty-two mean? Five minutes' reflection should tell any reasonable person that the man was overworking himself, and going at a pace no man could hold and live. Does not this show a lack of sense, and especially when much of that work could certainly have been done by subordinates? Was not one of Daniel Webster's best points his skill in getting work done by others, and saving for himself the parts he liked best?

When, after long years of toil and perseverance, one has worked himself up to position and wide influence, is it sensible to do what his humblest employé could rightly tell him is overcrowding, and so forcing the pace that he certainly cannot hold it? Instead of taking that position and that influence and wielding them for greater ends, and improving them very markedly, must there not be a keen pang to their owner when, tantalized with what seems surely within his grasp, that grasp itself weakens, and the machine goes all to pieces?

These later years are especially the precious ones to the wealthy man. They are his best days. Then his savings, and his earnings too, accumulate as they did not when he was younger. Look at the work done by Vanderbilt, for example, accomplished almost thirty years after he was fifty-two! Did not the active out-door life on the little periauger of his youth, and the daily constitutionals which, notwithstanding his infirmities, all New Yorkers saw him taking in later life, pay him? And are they less precious in any other line of life?

Look for a moment at the value health is to a man in any of the learned professions—of having a sound and vigorous body, with each branch of his vital system working regularly, naturally, and in harmony with the rest. Do these things make no difference to the divine? Had the sturdy, prize-fighter make of Martin Luther nothing to do with his contempt for the dangers awaiting his appearance before Charles V. and his Diet of Worms, and which caused him to say he would go there though the devils were as thick as the tiles on the houses; and with the grand stand he made for the religious light which now shines so freely upon the whole Christian world?

Thomas Guthrie, first tying one hand behind him, with the other could whip any man in Oxford who would also fight one-handed. Who doubts that the vigor so evinced had much to do with the faithful, arduous life's work he did, and did so well that all Scotland is to-day justly proud of him?

Have the magnificent breadth and depth of Spurgeon's chest, and his splendid outfit of vital organs, no connection with his great power and influence as a preacher of world-wide renown? Have the splendid physique and abounding vitality of Henry Ward Beecher—greater almost than that of any man in a hundred thousand—nothing to do with his ability to attend to his duties as pastor, author, lecturer, and editor—work enough to kill half a dozen ordinary men—and with the tireless industry which must precede his marked success in them all? Are not the towering form, the ruddy health, and grand, manly vigor of Dr. John Hall weighty elements, first in putting together, and then in driving home, the honest, earnest, fearless words which all remember who ever heard him speak? Have not the great bodies of those two young giants of the American pulpit, Phillips Brooks and Joseph Cook, proved most valuable accessories to their great brains?

Is there anything feeble about any of these? Put the tape-measure around them anywhere you like, and see how generous nature has been with them. Is it all a mere chance that they happen to have splendid bodies? Why is it that we never hear of such as these having "ministers' sore throat," and "blue Mondays," and having to be sent by their congregations, every now and then, away to a foreign land to recruit their health and keep them up to their work? Do sound and sturdy bodies, and due attention daily to keeping them in good repair, have nothing to do with their ability to cope at all times with the duty lying next to them—and with their attention to it, too, in such a way as to make them so much more effective than other men in their great life's work?

That the physician himself needs sound health and plentiful strength, few will question; and yet, does he, from his calling alone, do anything to insure it? Dragged from his bed at all hours of the night, thrown daily, almost hourly, in contact with deadly disease—often so contagious that others shrink from going where he goes, like the brave man he must be to face such dangers— would not that general toned-up condition of the thoroughly sound and healthy man prove a most valuable boon to him—indeed, often save his life? And yet, does his daily occupation insure him that boon, even though it does enable him to get out-of-doors far more than most men who earn their living by mental labor? Witness one of their own number, Dr. Mitchell, on this point; for he says, "The doctor, who is supposed to get a large share of exercise, in reality gets very little after he grows too busy to walk, and has then only the incidental exposure to out-door air." Would not a sensible course of physical exercise daily pay him—especially when pretty much all the muscular work he gets of any account is for his forearms and a little of his back, and then only when he drives a hard-bitted horse?

And does not a lawyer need a good body, and one kept in good order? After the first few years, when his practice is once well established, he finds that, unlike men in most other callings, his evenings are not his own, and that, if he is going to read any law, and to attempt to keep up with the new decisions every year, even in his own State, what between court work, the preparation of his cases, drawing papers, consultation, correspondence, and the other matters which fill up the daily round of the lawyer in active practice, that reading will have to be done out of office-hours often, or not done at all. Even in his evenings his business is too pressing to allow any time for reading. Here, then, is a man who is in serious danger of being cut off from that rest and recreation which most other men can have. The long, steady strain, day and evening, often breaks him down, where an hour's active exercise daily on the road or on the water, with his business for the time scrupulously forgotten, together with from a quarter to half an hour, on rising and retiring, in strengthening his arms and chest, would have kept him as tough and fresh as they did Bryant, not simply up to sixty, or even seventy, but clear up to his eighty-fourth year. Every lawyer who has been in active practice in any of our large cities for a dozen years can point to members of his Bar who have either broken clean down, and gone to a premature grave from neglecting their bodily health, or who are now far on the road in that same direction. This happens notwithstanding the fact that in many places the courts do not sit once during the whole summer, and lawyers can hence get longer vacations and go farther from home than most men.

Let any one read the life of Rufus Choate, and say whether there was any need of his dying an old man at fifty-five. He started not with a weak body, but one decidedly strong. So little care did he take of it that, as he himself well put it, "latterly he hadn't much of any constitution, but simply lived under the by-laws." Did it hinder his distinguished compeer, Daniel Webster, from magnificent success at the bar because he took many a good play-spell with a fishing-rod in his hand? because he not only knew but regarded the advantage and wisdom of keeping his body toned-up and hearty, and so regarded it that he died, not at fifty-five, but at the end of the full threescore years and ten? And did grand physical presence, the most impressive which ever graced American forum or senate-chamber—so striking, in fact, that, as he walked the streets of Liverpool, the laboring men stopped work and backed their admiring gaze by concluding that he must be a king—did these qualities not contribute to that same magnificent success? Daniel O'Connell was a man of sturdier body even than Webster, of whom Wendell Phillips says: "He was the greatest orator that ever spoke English. A little O'Connell would have been no O'Connell. Every attitude was beauty, every gesture grace. There was a magnetism that melted every will into his."

Had not this wonderful man much to thank these same qualities for? Had they not something to do with the stretching of his vigorous life, not merely up to fifty-five, or even to seventy, but clear up to seventy-three? How many men has the world ever seen who filled, and well filled, more high offices than Henry Brougham, and who, no matter where he was, was always a tireless worker? One biographer says that, as a boy, he was the fleetest runner in the neighborhood, and this man, "as an orator, second in his time only to Canning;" this man, who once spoke in Parliament for seven days consecutively, who, even when upward of seventy, showed his zeal for reform by urging the introduction into England of the New York Code of Procedure —this one of England's most famous Lord Chancellors took such care of his body that he never ceased from his labors until he was eighty-nine.

Let us look at but one more instance of the way a powerful mind and an uncommonly strong body blend and aid their possessor to his purposes. A recent writer in "Blackwood" says of Bismarck: *"He is a powerful man. That is what strikes at once every one who sees him for the first time. He is very tall and of enormous weight, but not ungainly. Every part of his gigantic frame is well-proportioned—the large round head, the massive neck, the broad shoulders, and the vigorous limbs. He is now more than sixty-three, and the burden he has had to bear has been usually heavy; but though his step has become slow and ponderous, he carries his head high—looking down, even, on those who are as tall as himself—and his figure is still erect. During these latter years he has suffered frequent and severe bodily pain, but no one could look upon him as an old man, or as one to be pitied. On the contrary, everybody who sees him feels that Prince Bismarck is still in possession of immense physical power."*

And what holds good as to professional men in this respect of course will apply with equal force to busy brain-workers in any other line as well. It is nowhere claimed here that there have not been in many callings great men whose bodies were indifferent affairs, but endeavor has been made to show, not only that a great mind and a vigorous body can go together, but that the latter is, not to the man of unusual mental power alone, but to every man, a most valuable acquisition, and one that he should, if he does not possess it already, take prompt steps to secure, and then, once acquiring it, should use the means, as Bryant did, to retain it.

In the 1877-'78 annual report of Harvard College, President Eliot, who has been exceptionally well-placed to observe several thousand young men, and to know what helps and what hinders their intellectual progress, adds his valuable testimony to the importance of vigorous health and regular physical exercise to all who have, or expect to have, steady and severe mental work to do. Busy professional men may well heed his words. Speaking of the value of scholarships to poor but deserving young men, he says: "If sound health were one of the requisitions for the enjoyment of scholarships, parents who expected to need aid in educating their boys would have their attention directed in an effective way to the wise regimen of health; while young men who had their own education to get would see that it was only prudent for them to secure a wholesome diet, plenty of fresh air, and *regular exercise*. A singular notion prevails, especially in the country, that it is the feeble, sickly children who should be sent to school and college, since they are apparently unfit for hard work. The fact that, in the history of literature, a few cases can be pointed out in which genius was lodged in a weak or diseased body, is sometimes adduced in support of the strange proposition that physical vigor is not necessary for professional men. But all experience contradicts these notions. *To attain success and length of service in any of the learned professions, including that of teaching, a vigorous body is well-nigh essential.* A busy lawyer, editor, minister, physician, or teacher has need of *greater physical endurance* than a farmer, trader, manufacturer, or mechanic. All professional biography teaches that *to win lasting distinction in sedentary, indoor occupations, which task the brain and the nervous system, extraordinary toughness of body must accompany extraordinary mental powers.*"

CHAPTER VI.
HOME GYMNASIUMS.

ALL that people need for their daily in-door exercises is a few pieces of apparatus which are fortunately so simple and inexpensive as to be within the reach of most persons. Buy two pitchfork handles at the agricultural store. Cut off enough of one of them to leave the main piece a quarter of an inch shorter than the distance between the jambs of your bedroom door, and square the ends. On each of these jambs fasten two stout hard-wood cleats, so slotted that the squared ends of the bar shall fit in snugly enough not to turn. Let the two lower cleats be directly opposite each other, and about as high as your shoulder; the other two also opposite each other, and as high above the head as you can comfortably reach.

Again, bore into the jamb, at about the height of your waist, a hole as large as the bar is thick. Now work the auger farther into each hole, till it reaches the first piece of studding, and then an inch or so into that. Find how many inches it is from the jamb to the end of the bore in the studding, and cut the second fork handle in halves. Pass one half through the hole in the jamb, and set its end into the hole in the studding. Bore a similar hole in the other jamb directly opposite, and repeat the last-named process with its nearest studding-piece, and adjust remainder of the fork handle to it. Now cut enough off each piece of the handle to leave the distance between the two about eighteen inches. You have then provided yourself with a pair of bars on which you can try one of the exercises usually practised on the parallel bars, and that one worth almost as much as all the rest. (See Fig. 3.)

Fig. 3.

On the following page is a sketch of a pair of pulley-weights recently made, designed by Dr. Sargent, which are excellent. Their merits will be seen at a glance. Instead of the weights swaying sideways and banging against the boxes, as they are liable to do in the ordinary old-fashioned pulley-weight boxes, they travel in boxes, A A, between the rods B B. A rubber bed also prevents the weight from making a noise as it strikes the floor, while another capital feature is the arrangement of boxes, in which you may graduate the weight desired by adding little plates of a pound each, instead of the unchanging weight of the old plan.

Fig. 4.

One of these boxes, with its load, can easily be used as a rowing-weight, by rigging a pulley-wheel a few inches above the floor, and directly in front of the weight box, and then making the rope long enough to also pass under this pulley. A stick of the thickness of an oar handle can then be attached to the end of the rope. If the old-fashioned pulley-weights are preferred, as they are cheaper, long boxes take the place of these iron rods, and a common iron weight travels up and down in the boxes. At some of the gymnasiums—that of the Young Men's Christian Association in New York, for example—these weights, of various sizes, snaffles, ropes, and handles, can all be had, of approved pattern and at reasonable rates.

Here, then, we have a horizontal bar fitted for most of the uses of that valuable appliance, a pair of parallel bars, or their equivalent for certain purposes, a pair of pulling-weights, and a rowing-weight. Now, with the addition of a pair of dumb-bells, weighing at first about one twenty-fifth of the user's own weight, we have a gymnasium more comprehensive than most persons would imagine. Mr. Bryant was contented for forty years with less apparatus even than this, and yet look at the benefit he derived from it![D] The bar, cleats, and parallels ought to be made and put up for not over two dollars, and four or five dollars more will cover the cost of pulling-weights and gear on the old plan, unless a heavy rowing-weight is added, which can be had at five cents a pound, which is also the price of well-shaped dumb-bells.

Here is a gymnasium, then, under cover, rent free, exactly at hand, when one is lightly clad on rising or just before retiring, which takes up but little room, can hardly get out of order, which will last a dozen years. With these few bits of apparatus every muscle of the trunk, nearly all those of the legs, and all those of the arms, can, by a few exercises so simple that they can be learned at a single trying, be brought into active play. The bar in the upper place will be useful mainly for grasping, hanging, or swinging on by the hands, or for pulling one's self up until the chin touches it. In the lower place it enables one to perform very many of the exercises usual on the horizontal bar. The short bars or handles have scarcely more than one office, but that is one of the most important of all exercises for the weak-armed and the weak-chested. This exercise is the one called "dipping." The bars are grasped with the hands, the feet being held up off the floor; then, starting with the elbows straight, gradually lowering until the elbows are bent as far as possible, then rising till they are straight again, and so continuing.

The pulley-weights admit of a great variety of uses, reaching directly every muscle of the hand, wrist, arm, shoulder, chest, abdomen, the entire back and neck; while, by placing one foot in the handle and pulling the weight with it, several of the leg muscles soon have plenty to do, as is also the case with the rowing-weight. The field of the dumb-bells is hardly less extensive.

If but one of these pieces of apparatus can be had, the pulley-weights are the most comprehensive, and so the most important, though it is astonishing how closely the dumb-bells follow; and then they have the great advantage of being portable. Combine with the exercises you can get from all this apparatus those which need none at all, such as rising on the toes, hopping, stooping low, walking, running, leaping, and no more tools are needed to develop whatever muscles one likes. What special work will employ any particular muscle will be indicated later.

If the apparatus is only to be used by a man or boy, a striking-bag can be made of seven or eight pieces of soft calf-skin, so that the whole, when full of sawdust, shall be either round like a ball or pear-shaped, and shall be about fifteen inches in horizontal diameter. This should be hung on a rope from a hook screwed into one of the beams of the ceiling. This makes a valuable acquisition to the snug little home-gymnasium. For a person having a weak chest, and who aims to broaden and deepen that important region, perhaps no better and safer contrivance can be had than the one sketched in Fig. 8, on page 248.

The fact of having a few bits of apparatus close at hand, when one is lightly clad, will tend to tempt any one to get at them a little while morning and evening. If a parent wants children to use them, instead of placing the apparatus in his own room, the nursery, or an empty room where all can have ready access, would be better. Of course, in such case there should be additional weights, and dumb-bells suited to the age and strength of those who are to use them.[E] Indeed, by providing children at home with articles which they like to use, and the use of which brings much direct good, the nursery has a new value—greater, perhaps, when made the most of, than it ever had before. All the exercises needed to make children strong can be readily learned, as all of them are exceedingly simple. In another place these exercises will be indicated. The parent can then select those exercises he sees the child needs, and teach them in a few minutes, so arranging it as to get the children to exercise a certain time every day. As has been shown, the cost of all these appliances will not be nearly as much as a moderate doctor's bill, and quite as little as the patent gymnastic articles, which are so often praised, mostly by people who know little or nothing of other forms of exercise than those fitted to their own apparatus. A large beam, for instance, has been devised, with handles fastened by a contrivance above it, which is meant to restore the spine (when out of place) to its proper position. But there is scarcely anything it can accomplish which cannot readily be done on some one of these simple, old-fashioned, and far less cumbrous pieces of apparatus.

Again, in the large cities there are establishments where the chief and almost the sole exercise is with the lifting-machine. A person, standing nearly erect, is made to lift heavy weights often of several hundred, and even a thousand or more pounds. The writer, when a lad of seventeen, worked a few minutes nearly every day for six months on a machine of this kind; and while it seemed a fine thing to lift six hundred pounds at first, and over a thousand toward the end, there came an unquestioned stiffening of the back, as though the vertebræ were packed so closely together as to prevent their free action. There came also a very noticeable and abnormal development of three sets of muscles: those of the inner side of the forearm, the lower and inner end of the front thigh just above the knee, and those highest up on the back, branching outward from the base of the neck. With considerable other vigorous exercise taken at the same time, this heavy lifting still produced the most marked effect, so that the development caused by it was soon large, out of all proportion compared with that resulting from the other work.

Now, if it is the fact that they who practice on the "health lift" ordinarily take little or no other vigorous exercise, why is not this same partial development going to result? And if this is the case, is it not rather a questionable exercise, especially for those to whom it is so highly recommended—the sedentary—and even worse for those who stand at desks all day? We have seen it make one very stiff and ungainly in his movements, and it is natural that it should; for he who does work of the grade suited to a truck-horse is far more likely to acquire the heavy and ponderous ways of that worthy animal than he who spreads his exercise over all, or nearly all, his muscles, instead of confining it to a few, and who makes many vigorous and less hazardous efforts instead of a single mighty one. All the muscles of the arm, for instance, which are used in striking out, putting up a dumb-bell, or any sort of pushing, are wholly idle in this severe pulling—more so, even, than they are in the oarsman when rowing. Hence, unless they get even work, there will be loss of symmetry, one-sided development, and only partial strength.

Another popular piece of apparatus is the "parlor gymnasium;" and, though needlessly expensive, it is a surprisingly useful affair, if once one knows how to use it to the best effect. But it has some disadvantages which, while not conceded by its inventor, it is yet well enough to know. In its more elaborate and complete form it is called the "Parlor Rowing Apparatus," and is also described as "the most complete rowing apparatus in the world." In reality it is very poorly adapted to the oarsman's wants, and tends to get him into habits he should, if he wishes to be a good oar, be careful to refrain from. It is a matter of supreme importance in rowing to get a strong grip at the beginning of the stroke, and to put the weight on heavily then; while it is a glaring fault to do anything like jerking toward the end of the stroke. But with this parlor rowing-machine, instead of lifting a solid weight, as in the ordinary rowing-weight, a rubber strap, or, rather, two rubber straps, are simply stretched while the stroke is pulled, and then slackened to begin the next. The trouble is that the straps have to be pulled nearly half the length of the stroke before it begins to grow hard to pull, so that throwing one's weight on heavily at the beginning causes the rower to feel somewhat as he would if, in taking a stroke in a boat, his oar-blade had missed the water entirely, or as a boxer who unexpectedly beats the air. The better the beginning of a stroke is caught in the water, the more the fulcrum of water itself solidifies, and by so much more can the rower throw his weight on then, and at just the right time. The effect with the rubber straps is the very reverse; for, in throwing the weight on at the beginning, the straps do not offer enough resistance to have the desired effect, while they offer too much at the finish of the stroke. This same defect stands out plainly in some of the pushing exercises done with it, as well as in using it as a lifting-machine, making it necessary, for the latter purpose, not to catch hold of the handles at all, but, as we have seen the inventor himself do, somewhere toward the middle of the straps, else the knees would get entirely straightened before the tension became great, which would force the bulk of the work to be done with the hands. Great care must be taken, also, to have the bolts at the farther ends of these straps fastened very firmly into the wood-work, or wherever they are attached; for if, under a heavy pull, one of these bolts should work out, it would be in great danger of striking the performer in the eye or elsewhere with terrific force.

Still, with these few defects, this parlor rowing apparatus is an excellent contrivance, and, used intelligently and assiduously, ought to bring almost any development a person might reasonably hope for, though its range is hardly as wide as that of these few bits of house apparatus before named, when taken together. There is nothing novel about the latter, excepting Dr. Sargent's apparatus for the chest. All have been known for a generation or more. But the many uses of them are but little known, and their introduction into our homes and schools has hardly yet begun. Yet, so wide is the range of exercise one can have with them, and of exercise of the very sort so many people need; and so simple is the method of working them, so free, too, from danger or anything which induces one to overwork, and so inexpensive are they and easy to make, that they ought to be as common in our homes as are warm carpets and bright firesides. Every member of the family, both old and young, should use them daily, enough to keep both the home-gymnasium and its users in good working order.

CHAPTER VII.

THE SCHOOL THE TRUE PLACE FOR CHILDREN'S

PHYSICAL CULTURE.

BUT, well adapted as our homes are in many ways for the proper care and development of the body, there is one place which, in almost every particular, surpasses them in this direction, if its advantages are understood and fully appreciated, and that is the school. A father may so arrange his time that a brief portion of it daily can be regularly allotted to the physical improvement of the children, as John Stuart Mill's father did his for his son's mental improvement, and with such remarkable results. But most fathers, from never having formed the habit, will be slow to learn it, and their time is already so taken up that it will seem impossible to spare any. The mother, being more with the child, feels its needs and lacks the more keenly, and would gladly deny herself much could she assure her children ruddy health. But her day is also by no means an idle one, and, just when she could best spare half an hour, it is hardest to have them with her. Besides, in too many instances she is herself far from strong, and needs some one to point out to her the way to physical improvement more, even, than do her children.

There is a feeling that the child is sent to *school* to be educated, and that certain trained persons are paid to devote their time to that education. As they are supposed to bring the children forward in certain directions, this leads easily to the conclusion that they would be the proper persons to care for other parts of that education as well. Nor is this view so wide of the mark. The teacher has always a considerable number of scholars. He can encourage the slower by the example of the quicker; he can arouse the emulation, he can get work easily out of a number together, where one or two would be hard to move. If he rightly understood his power; if he knew how easy it is, by a little judicious daily work, to prevent or remove incipient deformity, to strengthen the weak, to form in the pupil the habit of sitting and standing erect, to add to the general strength, to freshen the spirits, and do good in other ways, he would gladly give whatever time daily would be necessary to the work, while, like most persons who try to benefit others, he would find that he himself would gain much by it as well. He has not a class of pupils stiffened by long years of hard overwork of some muscles, and with others dormant and undeveloped. The time when children are with him is almost the best time in their whole lives to shape them as he chooses, not morally or mentally only, but physically as well. The one shoulder, a little higher than its mate, will not be half so hard to restore to place now as when confirmed in its position by long years of a bad habit, which should never have been tolerated a day. If the chest is weak and flat, or pigeon-breasted, now is the time to remove the defect. Build up the arms to be strong and comely now; accustom the chest and shoulders to their proper place, whatever their owner is at; cover the back with full and shapely muscles; get the feet used to the work which comes so easy and natural to them, once they are trained aright; and the same boy who would have grown up half-built, ungraceful, and far from strong, will now ripen into a manly, vigorous, well-knit man, of sound mind and body, familiar with the possibilities of that body, with what is the right use and what the abuse of it, and knowing well how to keep it in that condition which shall enable him to accomplish the best day's mental labor. And he will be far fitter to face the privations, anxieties, and troubles of life in the most successful way.

Nor is the rule at all difficult to follow. Little by little the boy's mind is led along, until the difficult problem in arithmetic seems no harder to him than did the adding of two and two at first. For hundreds of years the mental training of youth has been a matter of careful thought and study, and no effort is spared to secure the best advantages of all the teaching of the past. But with that past before him; with its many great men—not always, to be sure, but so often—men whose bodies were sturdy, and equal to the tremendous tasks which their great activity of mind led them willingly to assume, he is encouraged and urged to keep his mind under continual pressure for many hours daily, and every incentive is brought to make the most of him in this direction. And yet that which would have helped him in almost every step he took, which would have fitted him to stand with ease what now in a few years so often breaks him down, is totally ignored and left quite out of sight.

It is plainly no fault of his. The blame lies with the system which, for generations together, has gone along so blindly. The life a farmer's son leads makes him strong and hearty, and when his school-days are over his work is of such a sort as to maintain all his vigor. The city lad who plays on the brick sidewalks, born often of half-developed parents, has no daily tasks which bring his muscles into vigorous play, strengthening his digestion. Is there any possible reason why the city lad should be favored physically like the country boy? The first has every incentive for daily exercise, the latter none at all.

There ought to be no more delay in this matter of physical education in the schools. Prompt and vigorous steps should be taken to acquaint every school-teacher in this country with such exercises as would quickly restore the misshapen, insure an erect carriage, encourage habits of full breathing, and strengthen the entire trunk and every limb. If the teachers have not the requisite knowledge now, let it at once be acquired. They, of all persons, are expected to know how to acquire knowledge, and to aid others in doing the same. As soon as they have gained even partial knowledge of how to effect these things, let them lose no time in imparting that knowledge to the pupil.

Physical education ought to be made compulsory in every school in this land. Have it directly under the eye and guidance of the teacher, and have that teacher know that, at the quarterly or semi-annual examinations, reasonable progress will be expected in this department just as certainly as in any other, and if he is not up to his work, that some one who is will be put in his place. Then that progress will surely come. It has come already, where the means have been understood and used, as witness Maclaren abroad and Sargent here; and it brings such a benefit to the pupil that no pains should be spared to insure it.

Scarcely a week passes but the press of our larger cities repeats the story of some overworked man or woman breaking completely down with general debility, the body not only a wreck, but too often the mind as well. Had that body been early shaped, and hardened, and made vigorous—as, for instance, Chief-justice Marshall's father looked to it that his great son's was—and the habit formed of taking daily work, and of the right sort to keep it so, and had the importance of that care been impressed on the mind till it had fixed itself as firmly as the sense of decency or the need of being clean, is it likely that the person would have allowed himself to get so run down, or, if he did, to remain so?

The trouble usually is that the man does not know what to do to tone himself up and keep himself equal to his tasks, or that it needs but a little to effect this. He will spend money like water; he will travel fast and far; he will do almost anything, but he knows no certain cure. Is it not as important to have good health and strength as to figure or write correctly, to read the Æneids or Homer, to pick up a smattering of French or German? Who is the more likely, if his life be in-door and sedentary, not to live half his days—he who has never learned to build and strengthen his body, and keep it regulated and healthy, and to know the value of that health, or he who has?

Is not work which will almost surely lengthen one's life, and increase his usefulness, worth doing, especially when it takes but a very little while daily to do it, and less yet when the habit commenced in childhood? Go through our public and private schools, and see how few thoroughly well-built boys and girls there are. Good points are not scarce, but how small the proportion of the deep-chested, the well-made and robust, who give good promise of making strong and healthy men and women! Fortunately there is nothing really difficult in the work of strengthening the weak, making the somewhat crooked straight, of symmetrizing the partially developed; indeed, on the other hand, it is, when once understood, simple, inexpensive, and easy. More than all this, it is a work which the teacher will find that almost every scholar will take hold of, not, as in many other branches, with reluctance, but with alacrity; and it is always pleasant teaching those who are eager to learn.

But a little time each day is needed, never over half an hour of actual work in-doors and an hour out-of-doors. Suppose a teacher has forty pupils, and that thirty of them have either weak or indifferent chests. Let her form a chest-class out of the thirty, and, for ten minutes a day, let them practice exercises aimed exclusively to enlarge and develop the chest. Some of such exercises will be pointed out on page 245. Begin very gradually, so mildly that the weakest chest there shall have no ache or pain from the exercise. For the first week do that same work, and that much of it daily, and no more; but do it carefully, and do not miss a stroke. Let this exercise come at the appointed hour, as certainly as any other study. The second week make the work a trifle harder, or longer, or both. In this, and in every exercise, insist, as far as possible, on an erect carriage of the head and neck, and frequently point out their value. Insist, further, on the pupil's always inhaling as large, and full, and slow breaths as he can, seeing to it that every air-cell is brought into vigorous play. Be careful that he or she does not, without your knowledge, get hold of heavier apparatus, or try more difficult exercise in the same direction, before the muscles are trained to take it. Overdoing is not only useless, and sure to bring stiffness and aches, but it is in it that any danger lies, never in light and simple work, adapted to the pupil's present strength, and done under the teacher's eye, or in heavier work after he has been trained gradually up to it. Now, when a fortnight has gone by, use a little heavier weights; stay at the work without weights a little longer, or draw the pulley-weight a few more strokes daily, never forgetting to hold the head and neck erect.

Will dumb-bells and weight-boxes be necessary? Yes, or their equivalents. If the former cannot be had, flat-irons or cobble-stones of the same weight will do pretty well, and sand-bags can be used in the weight-boxes when pear-shaped weights or packed-boxes are scarce. It is a very small matter to supply a school with light dumb-bells, when they cost but five cents a pound, and when, if necessary to retrench, a quarter as many pairs of them as there are scholars will suffice. As will be shown in a later chapter, there is a very wide variety of exercises which could be practised in a school-room, which do not need one cent's worth of apparatus. They simply need to be known, and then faithfully practised, and most gratifying results are sure. In large cities it would be well to have all the teachers instructed by a competent master in the various exercises which they could so readily teach in school, and which would prove so beneficial to the scholars. London is already ahead of us in this direction. *Harper's Weekly* of February 8th, 1879, says: "The London School Board has appointed Miss Lofving, at a salary of fifteen hundred dollars a year, as superintendent of 'physical education' in the girls' schools."

A man like Dr. Sargent, of the Fifth Avenue Gymnasium, in New York, could easily, in a few half-hour lessons, instruct the two thousand or more teachers of the public schools of that city in the simpler, and yet very valuable exercises. They would be then well qualified, in turn, to instruct all the pupils, and to so grade their exercises as to adapt the work to all. The ordinary gymnastic instructor, as years have shown, in most of our gymnasiums, lets the pupil do about as he has a mind to. This would be just about as effective as if the same rule was followed out in mental training. But men like Sargent, strict disciplinarians, trained physicians, and practical gymnasts as well, are far too scarce among us, and his is a field which many of our young physicians might enter with prospects of doing very great good in the community in which they live.

Let the school commissioners of each State look to this matter at once. Let them insist that each teacher shall forthwith obtain the knowledge requisite to properly instruct and bring forward every pupil in his or her class. A knowledge should be had of the exact kind and amount of work requisite for a class of a certain age. Let some suitable person or persons be appointed in the cities to supervise this branch of education, and see that the teachers are thoroughly qualified. Let the scholar understand that his body can be trained exactly as well as his mind, and that the sound health of both is intimately connected with having it so trained. Let the school-hours be so arranged that ten minutes in the middle of the morning session, and again in the afternoon, shall be allotted to this branch. See what Maclaren[F] did for the Radley and Magdalen boys in *one hour a week!* see what Sargent[G] did in our country for two hundred youth in two hours a week, and with wooden dumb-bells, very light clubs, and a few pulley-weights at that! Let people at once and forever get rid of the notion that this exercise is a mere play-spell, or that it is only good to make athletes or acrobats. It is as much a branch of education as any taught in our schools to-day; and who will question that, if such uniform and splendid progress was made in each school as was made in the cases just cited, and in different instances, with at first such unpromising pupils, the brief twenty minutes daily so spent would be as well spent and as valuable to each pupil as any other twenty or thirty minutes of his day? It should no more be allowed to interfere with their usual play than any other branch is. It is a matter of progress and development, in a way highly important to every scholar, and should be so treated, and the child's play-hours should be in no way curtailed to accomplish it.

Superintendent Philbrick, of the Boston schools, is a man of long experience in most matters connected with schools, their management, and wants. This gentlemen has lately received, at the Paris Exposition, high honor for his accomplishments in this direction. But are the schools of Boston to-day taking the care they ought to and could so easily take to make the children healthy and vigorous? Let Mr. Philbrick set about introducing into every public school in that city such a system of physical education as shall effect, for example, simply what Maclaren effected, what Sargent effected and is now effecting, and no more. Let him stick to his task as persistently, if need be, as Stanley stayed at his infinitely harder one, until every boy or girl who is graduated from a Boston school has a strong, shapely, and healthy body, and knows what did much to make it so, and what will keep it so. Then the east wind may blow over that good city, even until no gilding remains on the State-house dome, and the formerly weak throats and lungs will not mind it any more than they do the gentlest southern zephyr; Mr. Philbrick can feel, when he looks over his life's work, that he has accomplished a thing for the scholars of his charge, and introduced a public benefit, which will redound to his credit as long as the city stands. There is no more need of Americans having poor legs than Englishmen. There is no more need of a boy's chest remaining a slim and half-built affair at the Brimmer School, or the Boston Latin School, than there was at Radley.

When the good work is commenced, when other cities begin to send their delegates and committees to watch methods, progress, and results, to take steps to secure the same benefits for their own schools, then the admirable example Boston has set in leading off in this direction will be better understood. Then all will wonder why so simple, so sensible, so effective a course, conducive to present and future health and well-being, had not been thought of and been carried out long ago.

CHAPTER VIII.
WHAT A GYMNASIUM MIGHT BE AND DO.

Few colleges of any pretension have not some sort of a gymnasium—indeed, hold it out to parents as one of the attractions. There is a building, and it has apparatus in it. The former often costs twice as much as needs be; the latter may be well made, and well suited to its purpose, or may not—in fact, more frequently is not. Instead of having apparatus graded, so as to have some for the slim and weak, some for the stout and broad, too often one pair of parallel bars or one size of rowing-weight must suffice for all. Frequently the apparatus getting loose, or worn, or out of repair, remains so. The director is little more than a janitor, and is so regarded. In many instances he does so little as to render this opinion a just one. Imperfect ventilation, and in winter lack of proper warmth, help to make it unattractive. The newly-arrived Freshman is generally run down and thin from overwork in preparing himself for college. Many a time, when much work was telling on him, he consoled himself with the thought that in the college-gymnasium, with his fellow-students about him all eagerly at work, he would soon pick up the strength he had lost, and perhaps come to be, in time, as strong as this or that fellow, a few years his senior, the fame of whose athletic exploits was more than local.

As a rule, the American student is not very strong on entering college. President Eliot, of Harvard, said, a few years ago, of a majority of those coming into that university, for instance, that they had "undeveloped muscles, a bad carriage, and an impaired digestion, without skill in out-of-door games, and unable to ride, row, swim, or shoot."

The student is usually inerect, and really needs "setting up" quite as much as the newly-arrived "pleb" at West Point. But does he get it? No. If coming from good stock, stronger than the average, and it happens to be a year when there is much interest in athletics, the rowing-men or the base-ball or foot-ball fellows will be after him. If they capture him, he will get plenty of work—more than enough—but in one single rut. If he knows something of the allurements of these sports, and desires to steer clear of them and be a reading man, still not to neglect his body, he is at a loss how to go to work. He finds a house full of apparatus, and does not know how to use it. He sees the boating and ball men hard at it, but on their hobbies, and looks about for something else to do. He finds no other class of fellows working with any vim, save those eager to show well as gymnasts. He falls in with these, takes nearly as much work the first day as they do, which is ten times too much for him, quite out of condition as he is. He becomes sore all over for two or three days, has no special ambition, after all, to be a gymnast, and, ten to one, throws up the whole business disgusted.

In the warmer months even the oarsmen and ball-players work out-of-doors, and, except a little brush by the new-comers during the first month or so, he finds the place deserted. At the start there was nobody to receive him, place him, and to encourage and invite him on. If naturally persistent, and he sticks to it awhile, he gropes about in a desultory way, now trying this and now that, until, neither increasing in size nor strength so fast as he had expected, he prefers to spend his spare hours in more attractive fields, and so drops the gymnasium, as many have done before him.

He has no more given it a fair trial than he would have his chemistry had he treated it in the same way. It is not his fault, for he knew no better. The whole method of bringing up most American boys does almost nothing to fit the average boy for even the simpler work of the gymnasium, let alone its more advanced steps. Often, in the university gymnasium, you will see fellows actually so weak in the arms that they can hardly get up in the parallel bars and rest their weight on their hands alone, much less go through them clear to the other end. It is a pretty suggestive commentary on the way these establishments are conducted that the men so lamentably deficient are by no means all from the new-comers, but often those who have nearly completed their course.

Yet here is a school which, rightly used, would do the average student more good, and would fit him better for his life's duties, than any other one branch in the whole curriculum.

But a few years since a son of a lawyer of national reputation, a highly gifted youth, made a most brilliant record at one of our best known colleges. All who knew him conceded him a distinguished future; and yet he was hardly well out of college when he took away his life. Had there been a reasonable, sensible allowance of daily muscular work, had the overtaxed brain been let rest awhile, and vigor cultivated in other directions, the rank, the general average, might have been a trifle lower, but a most efficient man saved for a long and honorable life. And yet every college has men who are practically following this one's plan, overworking their brains, cutting off both ends of the night, forcing their mental pace, till even the casual observer sees that they cannot stand it long, and must break down before their real life's race is well begun. Now, however exceptional may be the talents such a man has, does not his course show either dense ignorance of how to take care of himself, or a lack of something which would be worth far more than brilliant talents—namely, common-sense?

Ought there not to be some department in a college designed to bring round mental development, where the authorities would step in and prevent this suicidal course? Oh, but there are such and such lectures on health. Yes, and in most instances you might as well try and teach a boy to write by merely talking to him, taking care all the time that he have no pen or pencil in his hand. It is a matter of surprise that college faculties are not more alive to the defects of the gymnasium conducted right under their very eyes. In every other branch they require a definite and specific progress during a given time, an ability to pass successfully periodical examinations which shall show that progress, and, if the pupil fails, it tells on his general standing, and is an element which determines whether he is to remain in college.

But in the gymnasium there is nothing of the sort, and in many cases the young man need not step into it once during the four years unless he likes. This state of things is partly accounted for by the fact that too many of the professors in our colleges do not know anything about a gymnasium, and what it can do for a man. Indeed, often, if from practical experience they were better up in this knowledge, it would beneficially affect the reputation of their college as a live institution.

Nor is the director, with very few exceptions, the right sort of man for his place. Either the faculty have no conception what they do need here, or they effectually drive off the man they ought to have by starving him. Professors' salaries are generally small enough, but the director of the gymnasium seldom gets half so much as the poorest paid of his brother professors. Indeed, the latter do not regard him as an equal at all, and until they do so with good reason, there is little prospect of improvement in this direction. A doctor as ill up to his work as the average college gymnasium director would soon be without a patient.

Nor are the gymnasiums of our cities and towns much better off. New York city to-day, with one or two exceptions, is utterly without a gymnasium worthy of her. Two of the best known are situated, one far below the street level, the other directly over a stable, and formerly at least, if not still, a very redolent stable at that. There is generally plenty of apparatus, most of which is good enough; but the boy or man who comes to use it finds at once the same things wanting as does the student in the college gymnasium. If he can already raise a heavy dumb-bell over his head with his right hand, he may, and often does, go on increasing his power in this single direction, but in years actually gains little or no size or strength in his other arm, his legs, or any other part of his body. No one stops him, or even gives him an idea of the folly of his course; indeed, no one has the power to do so. Ordinarily the place is kept by a man simply to make a living. This secured, his ambition dies. He may be a boxer or an acrobat, or even a fair general gymnast. With one or two exceptions, we have yet to hear of an instance where the instructor has either devised a plan of class exercise which has proved attractive, or in a given time has brought about a decided increase in size and strength to a majority of his pupils in a specific and needed direction.

College rowing and base-ball, while often unquestionably benefiting those who took part in them, have been found to work detrimentally, but in a way, as will be shown in a moment, certainly not expected by the public. The colleges in this country which pay most attention to rowing are Harvard, Yale, Cornell, and Columbia. It is well known that in both Oxford and Cambridge universities the men who row are numbered by hundreds; that over twenty eight-oared crews alone, to say nothing of other classes, are sometimes on the river at once, and that the problem for the "'Varsity" captain is not, as here, to find eight men all fitted for places in the boat, but, out of many fit, to tell which to take. For years the American press has reported the performances of our student oarsmen even oftener and more fully than the English non-sporting papers those of their own oarsmen, so that they have filled a larger space in the public eye. Men naturally thought that the interest among the students themselves was well-nigh universal, and many fathers expressed misgivings about sending sons to institutions where the regular curriculum seemed a secondary matter, and performance in athletic contests the chief thing.

Yet, strange as it may seem, this whole idea is an egregious mistake. Most of the students do take some interest in these contests, but it goes no farther than talking somewhat about them, and viewing them when they come off, and perhaps betting the amount of their term-bills on them. The number who actually take part, either in the racing or the ball matches, or in trying for a chance in them, is ridiculously small. Dr. Sargent says that at Yale College, where he has been for six years instructor in physical culture, they actually do not exceed three per cent. of the whole number of students, while five per cent. will include every man in college who takes active work at the gymnasium, on the river, or the ball-field! Any one familiar with American college athletics knows that the proportion of students who either play ball or row is probably, taking year and year together, about as great at Yale as anywhere in the country.

Surprising as these figures are, they prove conclusively that the present system of college athletics, so far as it assumes to benefit the students at large, or even a tithe of them, is an utter failure. Here, then, instead of the supposed advance in the general physical culture over that of years ago, there has been almost no advance. There are a few men who devote much time and attention to severe athletics, more than there is any need of, and become skilled and famous at them, but the great majority do little or nothing. Better ideas they doubtless have of what is and what is not creditable performance among the athletes, and also as to the progress that can be made in muscular development by direct and steady work. But that progress and that work they have no share in.

The very natural result follows, that the great majority of students, at graduation, average no better in size, strength, health, vigor, endurance, or stamina than those of a generation ago, or are any fitter to stand successfully the wear and tear of their life's work. Indeed, it is very doubtful if they are physically as well fitted for what is before them as the previous generation were, for in the latter case probably more came from farms and homes where much manual labor was necessary, while now a greater fraction are from the cities, or are the sons of parents whose occupation is mainly sedentary. Yet in that day gymnasiums at the colleges were almost unknown, while now they are general.

Does the gymnasium, then, pay? Yes, like a bath-tub—if used, and used sensibly; but if not, not. Then, as it is used so little, is it worth having?

At Harvard, for instance, to-day there is in process of erection, at great expense, a gymnasium which, when finished, will doubtless be the most costly building of the sort in this country, and very possibly the best appointed as well. But unless there is introduced some sensible and vigorous system of bringing the students regularly there, and working them while they are there, it will almost surely prove a failure, and accomplish little or no more good than did the old one. Now, suppose, first that this new institution is to be carried on with no more vigor or good sense than its predecessors. Next, suppose that, opposite this expensive affair, on some neighboring field, there were built a commodious shed, costing perhaps one-tenth as much as its more pretentious rival, strongly framed, weather-tight, sensibly arranged, well lit, and comfortably warmed, large enough, too, to admit, at the edge of the main room, of a running track of say twenty laps to the mile. In an L adjoining let there be ample and well-ventilated dressing-rooms, a locker for each student, and sufficient washing facilities to meet the demand. Suppose the ordinary sorts of apparatus were there, but made with great care, and of the proportions skilled gymnasts have found most suitable. Let there be, besides, all newly-invented appliances which have proved valuable, such as the twenty or more Dr. Sargent has introduced, and any other good ones as well. Suppose, too, that heavy weights for lifting, and all heavy clubs and dumb-bells, were carefully excluded.

On the walls there should be casts and drawings, showing well-proportioned and well-developed arms, legs, and trunks, and a brief statement with each of the various measurements and proportions, and the ages of the men from whom they were taken, and, if possible, the sort and amount of work done by each in their progress. These need by no means be all modern. Greece and Rome, Troy and Pompeii, could furnish their quota.

Suppose the director at once, on the joining of a pupil, recorded, on a page set apart specially in his register, the age, height, general physical characteristics, weight, girth of calf, thigh, hips, waist, lower chest, upper chest—both at rest and inflated—neck, upper arm—extended and drawn up—and the forearm, hand, and wrist, taking care to note the time of day the measurements were made, and also obtaining a photograph of the man as he then appeared in exercising costume. Suppose that, outside of the ordinary requirements as to method, decorum, order of using apparatus, and so on, the director refused to take any pupil who would not expressly agree to two things: first, to be at the gymnasium, stripped and ready for work, exactly at such a moment, four days out of the seven; second, to obey implicitly the director's orders, both as to what work he should do, and what omit.

Suppose the director's training had been such that he could tell at once, both from the looks and measurements of the man, where he was physically lacking, and that he so arranged his classes that all whose left hands were weaker than their right had left-handed work only until they were equalized up; that weak thighs, calves, abdominal muscles, chests, and backs had special work given them, bringing the desired parts directly into play, lightly as each needed at first, and then gradually working upward, the stronger parts, meanwhile, being at rest. Suppose this were continued until, at the end of the year, or often long before it, it is found that one arm is now as strong as the other, that the gain in girth at almost every measurement is nearly or all of an inch, and at some even two or more inches.

Suppose a series of exercises, aimed directly to enlarge and strengthen the respiratory power, were given to all, and every one, also, had a few minutes each day of "setting up," and other work aimed not so much to add size and strength as to make the crooked straight, to point out and insist on a proper carriage of the head, the neck, the shoulders, the arms, the whole trunk, and the knees, and to show each pupil what length of step best suited him, and which he ought to take.

Suppose that the director showed at once that he not only knew what to do all through, but how to do it, and so promptly won the confidence of those he sought to instruct and benefit.

Is there any question in which of these two institutions the young man would make the most desirable progress? The first building and apparatus might be grand, fitted up with nearly all that could be desired, but the gymnasium lacked a masterhead who should show its possibilities. Gymnasium and apparatus were like an engine without steam. The second building was not of much account as a building, but quite all that was needed for the real end in view. The London Rowing-club boat-houses were for a long time mere sheds, not to be named in the same day with the tasteful stone boat-houses along the Schuylkill, for instance; but those same plain sheds have for many years turned out amateur oarsmen who could row down any in the world.

And what a benefit a gymnasium conducted on some plan similar to that above suggested would be to any college or university! And yet almost any college, even of limited means, could afford it. Change the plan a little, and make the attendance by all students just as it is in other branches—just as it is at West Point in horseback practice—compulsory. Give the director a salary adequate to secure a first-class man in his calling—not merely an accomplished gymnast, acrobat, boxer, or fencer, but an educated physician, the peer of any of his brother-members of the faculty, fond of his calling, fond of the field before him, thoroughly acquainted with the plainer kinds of gymnastics and of acrobatic work, and a good boxer, an instructor especially quick in detecting the physical defects in his pupil, in knowing what exercise will cure them, zealous in interesting him, in encouraging him on, what incalculable good he could do! Every student in that college would practically have to be made over. Long before the four years, or even one of them, were through, that instructor would have made all the men erect (as is daily being done with the West Pointer). But his pupils, instead of being like the latter, developed simply in those muscles which his business called into play, would each be well developed all over, would each be up to what a well-built man of his years and size ought to be in the way of strength, and skill, and staying powers, and—a most important thing—would know what he could do, and what he could not; and so would not, as is now every day the case with many, attempt physical efforts long before he was fitted for them.

If he wanted to go into racing, the director would be his best friend, and would point out to him that the only safe way to get one's heart and lungs used to the violent action which they must undergo in racing, especially after the racer gets tired, would be by gradually increasing his speed from slow up to the desired pace, instead of, as too often happens, getting up to racing pace before he is half fit for it.

But he would also show him how one-sided it would make him, developing some parts, and letting others remain idle and fall behind in development, and

—more important still—how brief and ephemeral was the fame which he was working for, and the risks of overdoing which it entailed.

Let one college in this land graduate each year a class of which every man has an erect carriage and mien, has the legs and arms, the back and chest, not of a Hercules, not of a prize racer or fighter, but of a hale, comely, strong, and well-proportioned man, and see how well it would pay. Bear in mind that an hour a day put in in the right way and at the right work will effect all this in far less time than four years of trying. The hardest-reading man can readily spare the time for it, especially if he must. What! would it take him from the thin, cadaverous fellow he too often is, and do all that for him? Beyond all doubt it would. Such vigorous work would soon sharpen his appetite, and he would find that, eat all he liked, he could digest it promptly, and would feel all the better for his generous living. The generous living has fed muscles now vigorously used; they have been enlarged and strengthened: the legs, which never used to try to jump a cubit high, even, once in the whole year, now carry their owner safely over a four-rail fence, and perhaps another rail, or even two of them. The lungs, which were scarcely half expanded, now have every air-cell thoroughly filled for at least one entire hour daily—an excellent thing for weak lungs. Correct positions of standing, sitting, walking, and running being now well known and understood, the lungs get more air into them than formerly, even when their owner is at rest. Another effect of it all is shown in a decidedly more vigorous circulation, and the consequent exhilaration and buoyancy of spirits, no matter whether the work in hand is mental or physical.

But will not this hour's work dull him mentally? It may be proper to digress for a moment and see if it will. Of men who have done just this kind and amount of work, this work aimed at every part of the body, we find no record, simply because, as we have already shown, considerable as the increased interest is in physical culture and development, this plan of reaching all the parts and being just to all, has scarcely been tried. But abundant proof that some physical exercise will not dull the man, but even brighten him, can be had without difficulty. A moment's reflection will show that a mind ever on the stretch must, like a bow so kept, be the worse for it, and that the strain must be occasionally slacked. There are two ways of slacking it. Both the physician and experience tell us that nothing rests a tired brain like sensible, physical exercise, except, of course, sleep.

"When in active use," says Mitchell, "the thinking organs become full of blood, and, as Dr. Lombard has shown, rise in temperature, while the feet and hands become cold. Nature meant that for their work they should be, in the first place, supplied with food; next, that they should have certain intervals of rest to rid themselves of the excess of blood accumulated during their periods of activity; and this is to be done by sleep, and also by bringing into play the physical machinery of the body, such as the muscles—that is to say, by exercise which flushes the parts engaged in it, and so depletes the brain."[H]

Here, then, some physical exercise will rest his brain, and fit it for more and better work. But this does not necessarily imply so much as is called for in the hour. Happily, however, there is no lack of instances where work, quite as vigorous, though not as well directed, has accompanied mental work of a very high order, and to all appearances has been a help rather than a hinderance. Instead of one hour a day, Napoleon for years was in the saddle several hours almost daily, but we never heard that it clogged his mind. Charles O'Conor, always fond of long walks, is good at them to-day, and noticeably erect and quick of movement, though for weeks he once lay at death's door, and though he was born in 1804. James Russell Lowell, sturdy, broad, and ruddy, is said to never ride when he can walk, and he is nearly sixty. Gladstone's reputation as an axeman among the Hawarden oaks has reached our shores. Indeed, it is doubtful if there are many better *fellers* of his age in Europe, and he was born in 1809. Mr. M.H. Beebee, the present senior tutor at Cambridge University in England, who rowed at number two in the "'Varsity" eight against Oxford in '65, not only took the very highest university honor—a double-first—but a much higher double-first than even Gladstone had taken years before. The fencing, duelling, and hard riding of Bismarck's youth do not seem to have perceptibly dimmed his intellect, or to have unfitted it for enormous and very important work in later life.

And while the in-door work equalizes the strength, and takes care of the arms and chest, the hour's "constitutional" daily out-of-doors has an especial advantage, in that it insures at least that much out-of-door life and air. Dr. Mitchell says, "When exposure to out-of-door air is associated with a fair share of physical exertion, it is an immense safeguard against the ills of anxiety and too much brain-work. I presume that very few of our generals could have gone through with their terrible task if it had not been that they lived in the open air and exercised freely. For these reasons I do not doubt that the effects of our great contest were far more severely felt by the Secretary of War and the late President than by Grant or Sherman."

A recent, interesting, and wonderfully apt instance, more so than any of these, one going straight to the point, and as nearly as possible the equivalent of what we propose to urge later on all sedentary men, one where the proof comes directly from the gentleman's own pen, is that of the late Mr. Bryant, whose letter on the subject, written to a friend in 1871, will be found on page 169. With characteristic sturdiness, with no one to aid or guide him, he hit on a plan of work to be done, partly in his little home-gymnasium, and partly on the road, and stuck faithfully to it till well over fourscore, and at eighty-two he told the writer that he continued his exercise simply because it paid. His aim was to keep all his machinery in working order, and to prolong his life; and when he did die, at eighty-four, it was not from old age, not because his functions were worn out. With his usual vigor and energy when any writing was to be done, he had thrown himself into his work of preparing his address at the Mazzini celebration, till, tired and exhausted, the undue exposure to the hot sun and the resulting fall were too much for him, and these were what took him away.

But the plan here suggested will not only cover all he did, but more. Bryant does not seem to have cared for erectness, nor for a harmonious development of all the muscles. But had the amount of work he took been so directed, he might in youth have attained that harmony, and maintained it through life, as Vanderbilt maintained his erectness.

There need be little fear, then, that a right use of the gymnasium will overdo. No better safeguard against that could be had than a wise director, familiar with the capacities of his pupil, watching him daily, instilling sound principles, and giving him the very work he needs. Under such a tutor a young man who went to college, on receiving his degree, would, if his moral and mental duties were attended to, be graduated, not with an educated mind alone, but an educated body as well; not with merely a bright head, and a body and legs like a pair of tongs. If the history of brave, independent, earnest, pure men goes for anything, it will be found that as the body was healthy and strong, it has in many a pass in life directly aided moral culture and strength, and has kept the man from defiling that body which was meant to be kept sacred.

CHAPTER IX.

SOME RESULTS OF BRIEF SYSTEMATIC EXERCISE.

IN a country like ours, where the masses are so intelligent, where so much care is taken to secure what is called a good education, the ignorance as to what can be done to the body by a little systematic physical education is simply marvellous. Few persons seem to be aware that any limb, or any part of it, can be developed from a state of weakness and deficiency to one of fulness, strength, and beauty, and that equal attention to all the limbs, and to the body as well, will work like result throughout. A man spends three or four weeks at the hay and grain harvest, and is surprised at the increased grip of his hands, and the new power of arm and back. He tramps through forests, and paddles up streams and lakes after game, and returns wondering how three or four miles on a level sidewalk could ever have tired him.

An acquaintance of ours, an active and skilled journalist, says that he once set out to saw twenty cords of wood, he was a slight, weak youth. He found he had not enough strength or wind to get through one cut of a log—that he had to constantly sit down and rest. People laughed at him, and at his thinking he could go through that mighty pile. But they did not know what was in him; for, sticking gamely to his self-imposed task, he says that in a very few days he found his stay improving rapidly, that he did not tire half so easily, and, more than that, that there began to come a feeling over him—a most welcome one—of new strength in his arms and across his chest; and that what had at first looked almost an impossibility had now become very possible, and was before long accomplished. Now, what he, by his manliness, found was fast doing so much for his arms and chest, was but a sample of what equally steady, systematic work might have done for his whole body. Indeed, a later experience of this same gentleman will be in place here; for at Dr. Sargent's gymnasium in New York, in the winter of 1878-'79, he, though a middle-aged man, increased the girth of his chest *two inches and five-eighths in six weeks*! and this working but one hour a day; and he found that he could not only do more work daily afterward at his profession, but better work as well.

The youth who works daily in a given line at the gymnasium as much expects that, before the year is over, not only will the muscles used decidedly increase in strength, but in size and shapeliness as well, as he does that the year's reading will improve his mind, or a year's labor bring him his salary. It is an every-day expression with him that such a fellow "got his arm up to" fifteen, or his chest to forty-odd inches, and so on. He sees nothing singular in this. He knows this one, who in a short time put half an inch on his forearm, or an inch; that one, whose thigh, or chest, or waist, or calf made equal progress. Group and classify these gains in many cases, and note the amount of work and the time taken in each, and soon one can tell pretty well what can be done in this direction. Few of our gymnasiums are so kept that their records will aid much in this inquiry, simply because the instructor either has no conception of the field before him, or, if he has, for some reason fails to improve the opportunity.

Look at what Maclaren effected (as described by him in his admirable "Physical Education"), not with here and there an isolated case, but with both boys and men turned in on him by the hundred, and in all stages of imperfect development! Take it first among the boys. Under systematic exercise, W——, a boy at Radley College, ten years old in June, 1861, had, seven years later, increased in height from 4 feet 6¾ inches to 5 feet 10¾ inches, or a gain of 16 inches in all; in weight from 66 pounds—light weight for a ten-year-old boy—to 156 pounds; far heavier than most boys at seventeen; showing an advance of 90 pounds. His forearm went from 7¼ to 11¾ inches—very large for a boy of seventeen, and decidedly above the average of that of most men; his upper arm from 7½ inches to $13\frac{1}{8}$,—also far above the average at that age; while his chest had actually increased in girth from 26 inches—which was almost slender, even for a ten-year-old—to 39½ inches, which is all of two inches larger than the average man's.

His description of this boy was: "Height above average; other measurements average. From commencement, growth rapid, and sustained *with regular and uniform development*. The whole frame advancing to great physical power."

Another boy, H——, starting in June, 1860, when ten years old, 4 feet 6¼ inches high, and weighing 73 pounds—much heavier than the other at the start—in eight years gained 13½ inches, making him 5 feet 7¾ inches—of medium height for that age. He gained 71 pounds in the eight years, and at 144 pounds was better built than W—— at 156; for, though his forearm, starting at 8 inches, had become 11½, a quarter of an inch less than W——'s, yet his upper arm had gone from 8¾ to 13½ inches, or one-eighth of an inch larger, while his chest rose from 28¼ to 39 inches—within half an inch of the other's, though the latter was 3 inches taller.

He is described: "Height slightly above average; other measurements considerably above average. From commencement, *growth and development regular and continuous. The whole frame perfectly developed for this period of life.*"

S——'s case is far more remarkable. He was evidently very small and undersized. "Height and all other measurements *greatly* below average; the whole frame stunted and dwarfish. Advancement at first slight, and very irregular. Afterward rapid, and comparatively regular."

He only gained in height three-quarters of an inch from thirteen to fourteen, where W—— had gained $3^5/_8$ inches, and H—— $3^1/_8$ inches. Yet, from fifteen to sixteen, where W—— only went ahead half an inch, and H—— five-eighths of an inch, S—— actually gained 4 inches, which must have been most gratifying. His weight changes were even more noticeable. From twelve to fifteen W—— gained 58 pounds, and H—— 39, while all S—— could show was 12. But from fifteen to sixteen see how he caught up! Where W——made 11 pounds, and H—— 10, S—— made 22. Where W——'s chest went up 1 inch, and H——'s 1½ inches, S——'s went up 3 inches.

Now, how long did these boys work? As Maclaren says "*Just one hour per week!*"

What parent believes that any hour in that week was better spent—better for the comfort, for the welfare of the boy, or better in fitting him for future usefulness—or what nearly so well? Most boys waste that much time nearly every day.

Look, too, at the benefit to the boy in all his after-life. Indeed, does not this hour a week, in some instances, insure an after-life, and snatch not a few from an early grave? Had every slim, thin-chested man in America, and every slim, thin-chested boy who never lived to be a man, spent an hour weekly under such tutoring, from the age of ten to eighteen, would not the benefit to our land in working-power, in vigor and force, and comfort as well, have been incalculable? And had it, instead of one hour a week, been two or three, or even an hour a day, might not the results have been even more gratifying?

Professor Maclaren may well congratulate himself on such good results among the boys. But what has he done with men? Some years ago twelve non-commissioned officers, selected from all branches of the service, were sent to him to qualify as instructors for the British army. He says:

"They ranged between nineteen and twenty-nine years of age, between five feet five inches and six feet in height, between nine stone two [128] pounds and twelve stone six [174] pounds in weight, and had seen from ten to twelve years' service."

He carefully registered the measurements of each at the start, and at different times throughout their progress. He says:

"The muscular additions to the arms and shoulders, and the expansion of the chest, were so great as to have absolutely a ludicrous and embarrassing result, for, before the fourth month, several of the men could not get into their uniforms, jackets, and tunics, without assistance, and when they had got them on they could not get them to meet down the middle by a hand's-breadth. In a month more they could not get into them at all, and new clothing had to be procured, pending the arrival of which the men had to go to and from the gymnasium in their great-coats. One of these men gained five inches in actual girth of chest."

And he well adds: "Now who shall tell the value of these five inches of chest, five inches of additional space for the heart and lungs to work in?" Hardly five inches more of heart and lung room, though part of the gain must have been of course from the enlargement of the muscles on the side of the chest.

He also hit upon another plan of showing the change; for he says he had them "photographed, stripped to the waist", both at first and when the four months were over, and the change even in these portraits was very distinct, and most notably in the youngest, who was nineteen, for, besides the acquisition of muscle, there was in his case "a readjustment and expansion of the osseous framework upon which the muscles are distributed." Now let us look a little at the measurements and the actual changes wrought.

In the first place, this last instance settles conclusively one matter most important to flat-chested youth, namely, whether the shape of the chest itself can be changed; for here it was done, and in a very short time at that. Again, of these twelve men, in less than eight months every one gained perceptibly in height; indeed, there was an average gain of five-twelfths of an inch in height, though all, save one, were over twenty; and one man who gained half an inch was twenty-eight years old, while one twenty-six gained five-eighths of an inch! (Most people suppose they can get no taller after twenty-one.) All increased decidedly in weight—the smallest gain being 5 pounds, the average 10 pounds; and one, and he twenty-eight, and a five-feet-eleven man, actually went up from 149 pounds at the beginning, to 165 pounds in less than four months. It is not likely there was much fat about them, as they had so much vigorous muscular exercise. Every man's chest enlarged decidedly, the smallest gain being a whole inch in the four months, the average being $2\frac{7}{8}$ inches, and one, though twenty-four years old, actually gaining 5 inches, or over an inch a month. Every upper arm increased 1 inch, most of them more than that, and one 1¾ inches. As the work was aimed to develop the whole body, there is little doubt that there was a proportional increase in the girth of hips and thigh and calf.

Again, from the Royal Academy at Woolwich, Professor Maclaren took twenty-one youths whose average age was about eighteen, and in the brief period of four months and a half obtained an average advance of 1¾ pounds in weight, of 2½ inches in chest, and of 1 inch on the upper arm; while one fellow, nineteen, and slender at that, gained 8 pounds in weight, and 5¼ inches about the chest! Think what a difference that would make in the chest of any man, and a difference all in the right direction at that!

But the most satisfactory statistics offered were those of two articled pupils, one sixteen, the other twenty. In exactly one year's work the younger grew from 5 feet 2¾ inches in height to 5 feet 4¾ inches. He weighed 108 pounds on his sixteenth birthday; on his seventeenth, 129! At the start his chest girthed 31 inches; twelve months later, just 36! His forearm went up from 8 inches to 10 inches, and his upper arm from 9¼ inches to 11¼.

While the older gained but three-eighths of an inch in height, his weight went up from 153 pounds to 161½, his forearm from 11¼ inches to 12½—an unusually large forearm for any man—and his upper arm from 11¾ inches to 13¼, while his chest actually made the astonishing stride of from 34 inches to 40. Not yet a large arm, save below the elbow, not yet a great chest; five inches smaller, for instance, than Daniel Webster's, but greatly ahead of what they were a year earlier.

There is no mystery about the Maclaren method. Others might do it, perhaps not as well as he, for Maclaren's has been a very exceptional experience; still, well enough.

Look what Sargent did with a Bowdoin student of nineteen, as shown in Appendix IV. In four hours' work a week this student's upper arm went up 1½ inches—just the same amount as did Maclaren's student of twenty; his chest went up from 36½ inches to 40, while that of Maclaren's man went from 34 to 40; but it should be borne in mind that 36½ is harder to add 6 inches to in this kind of work than 34. In height the Englishman made three-eighths of an inch in the year, while the American made a whole inch. But the latter also led easily in another direction, and a very important one too; for, while the Briton, though but a year older, and of almost exactly the same height, gained but 8½ pounds in the year, the American made 15! His case is further valuable in that it shows, beside this advance above the waist, splendid increase in girth of hips, thigh, and calf as well.

With us Americans fond of results, many of whose chests, by-the-way, do not increase a hair's-breadth in twenty years, better proof could not be sought than these figures offer of the value of a system of exercise which would work such rapid and decided changes. Had they all been with boys, there might have been difficulty in separating what natural growth did, in the years they change so fast, from what was the result of development. But most of the cases cited are of men who had their growth, and had apparently, to a large extent, taken their form and set for life. To take a man twenty-eight years old, tall and rather slim, and whose height had probably not increased a single hairs-breadth in seven years, and in a few short months increase that height by a good half inch; to take another, also twenty-eight, and suddenly, in the short period between September 11th and the 30th of the next April, add sixteen pounds to his weight, and every pound of excellent stuff, was in itself no light thing; and there are thousands of men in our land to-day who would be delighted to make an equally great addition to their general size and strength, even in twice the period. To add five whole inches of chest, and nearly that much of lung and heart room and stomach room, and the consequent greater capacity for all the vital organs, is a matter, to many men, of almost immeasurable value. Hear Dr. Morgan, in his English "University Oars," on this point: "An addition of three inches to the circumference of the chest implies that the lungs, instead of containing 250 cubic inches of air, as they did before their functional activity was exalted, are now capable of receiving 300 cubic inches within their cells: the value of this augmented lung accommodation will readily be admitted. Suppose, for example, that a man is attacked by inflammation of the lungs, by pleurisy, or some one of the varied forms of consumption, it may readily be conceived that, in such an emergency, the possession of enough lung tissue to admit forty or fifty additional cubic inches of air will amply suffice to turn the scale on the side of recovery. It assists a patient successfully to tide over the critical stage of his disease." A man, then, of feeble lungs—the consumptive, for instance—taken early in hand, with the care which Maclaren or Sargent could so well give, gradually advanced in every direction, would suddenly find that his narrow, thin, and hollow chest had departed, had given way to one round, full, deep, and roomy; that the feeble lungs and heart which, in cooler weather, were formerly hardly up to keeping the extremities warm, are now strong and vigorous; that the old tendency to lean his head forward when standing or walking, and to sit stooping, with most of his vital organs cramped, has all gone. In their place had come an erect carriage, a firm tread, a strong, well-knit trunk, a manly voice, and a buoyancy and exhilaration of spirits worth untold wealth. Who will say that all these have not assured him years of life?

Well, but did all this increase of weight and size actually change the shape of the chest, for instance, and take the hollowness out of it? That is exactly what it did; and Maclaren has a drawing of the same chest at the beginning and end of the year, showing an increase in the breadth, depth, and fulness of the lower chest which makes it seem almost impossible that it could have belonged to the same person. It will be remembered that Maclaren claimed[1] that just such a readjustment of the osseous framework would result. Is not this, then, remaking a man? Instead of a cramped stomach, half-used lungs, a thin, scrawny, caved-in make, poor pipe-stems of legs, with arms to match, almost every one under forty, at least, can in a very few months, by means of a series of exercises, change those same slender legs, those puny arms, that flat chest, that slim neck, and metamorphose their owner into a well-built, self-sufficient, vigorous man, fitter a hundred times for severe in-door or out-door life, for the quiet plodding at the desk, or the stormy days and nights of the ocean or the bivouac. Who is going to do better brain-work: he whose brain is steadily fed with vigorous, rich blood, made by machinery kept constantly in excellent order, never cramped, aided daily by judicious and vigorous exercise, tending directly to rest and build him up? or he who overworks his brain, gets it once clogged with blood, and, for many hours of the day, keeps it clogged, who does nothing to draw the blood out of his brain for awhile and put more of it in the muscles, who, perhaps, in the very midst of his work, rushes out, dashes down a full meal, and hurries back to work, and at once sets his brain to doing well-nigh its utmost?

Well, but is not the work which will effect such swift changes very severe, and so a hazardous one to attempt? That is just what it is not. Is there anything very formidable in wooden dumb-bells weighing only two and a half pounds each, or clubs of three and a half-pounds, or pulley-weights of from ten to fifteen pounds? or is any great danger likely to result from their use? And yet they were Sargent's weapons with his Bowdoin two hundred.[1] Nothing in Maclaren's work, so far as he points out what it is, is nearly so dangerous as a sudden run to boat or train, taken by one all out of the way of running, perhaps who has never learned. There a heart unused to swift work is suddenly forced to beat at a tremendous rate, lungs ordinarily half-used are strained to their utmost, and all without one jot of preparation.

But here, by the most careful and judicious system, the result of long study and much practical application, a person is taken, and, by work exactly suited to his weak state, is gradually hardened and strengthened. Then still more is given him to do, and so on, at the rate that is plainly seen to best suit him. Develop every man's body by such a method, teach every American school-boy the erect carriage of the West Pointer, and how many men among us would there be built after the pattern of the typical brother Jonathan, or of the thin-chested, round-shouldered, inerect, and generally weak make, so common in nearly every city, town, and village in our land?

Look, too, at the knowledge such a course brings of the workings of one's own body, of its general structure, of its possibilities! What a lecture on the human body it must prove, and how it must fit the man to keep his strength up, and, if lost, to recover it; for it has uniformly been found that a man once strong needs but little work daily to keep him so. A little reflection on facts like the foregoing must point strongly to the conclusion that the body—at least of any one not yet middle-aged—admits of a variety and degree of culture almost as great as could be desired, certainly sufficient to make reasonably sure of a great accession of strength and health to a person formerly weak, and that with but a little time given each day to the work.

CHAPTER X.

WORK FOR THE FLESHY, THE THIN, THE OLD.

WHILE the endeavor has been made to point out the value of plain and simple exercise—for, in a later chapter, particular work will be designated which, if followed systematically and persistently, will correct many physical defects, substituting good working health and vigor for weakness—the reply may be made, "Yes, these are well enough for the young and active, but they will not avail a fleshy person, or a slim one, or one well up in years."

Let us see about this. Take, first, those burdened with flesh which seems to do them little or no good, and which is often a hinderance, dulling and slackening their energies, preventing them from doing much which they could, and which they believe they would do with alacrity were they once freed from this unwelcome burden. There are some persons with whom the reduction of flesh becomes a necessity. They have a certain physical task to perform, and they know they cannot have either the strength or the wind to get through with it creditably, unless they first rid themselves of considerable superfluous flesh.

Take the man, for instance, who wants to walk a race of several miles, or to run or row one. He has often heard of men getting their weight down to a certain figure for a similar purpose. He has seen some one who did it, and he is confident that he can do it. He sets about it, takes much and severe physical work daily, warmly clad, perspiring freely, while he subjects his skin to much friction from coarse towels. He does without certain food which he understands makes fat, and only eats that which he believes makes mainly bone and muscle. He sticks to his work, and gradually makes that work harder and faster. To his gratification, he finds that not only has his wind improved, so that, in the place of the old panting after a slight effort—walking briskly up an ordinary flight of stairs, for instance—he can now breathe as easily and quietly, and can stick to it as long, as any of his leaner companions. By race-day he is down ten, fifteen, or twenty pounds, or even more, as the case may be. While he has thus reduced himself, and is far stronger and more enduring than he was before, he is not the only one who has lost flesh, if there have been a number working with him, as in a boat-crew. Notice the lists of our university crews and their weights, published when they commence strict training, say a month before the race, and compare them with those of the same men on race-day, particularly in hot weather. The reduction is very marked all through the crew. In the English university eights it is even more striking, the large and stalwart fellows, who fill their thwarts, often coming down in a month an average of over a dozen pounds per man.

We have seen a student, after weighing himself on scales in the gymnasium, sit down at a fifty-five pound rowing weight, pull forty-five full strokes a minute for twenty minutes, then, clad exactly as before, weigh again on the same scales, and find he was just one pound lighter than he was twenty minutes earlier.

But the difference is more marked in more matured men, who naturally run to flesh, than in students. A prize-fighter, for instance, in changing from a life of indulgence and immoderate drinking, will often come down as much as thirty, or even forty pounds, in preparing for his contest. It should be remembered that, besides other advantages of his being thin, it is of great importance that his face should be so lean that a blow on his cheek shall not puff it up, and swell it so as to shut up his eye, and put him at his enemy's mercy.

But most people do not care to take such severe and arduous work as either the amateur athlete or the prize-fighter. If they could hit on some comparatively light and easy way of restoring themselves physically to a hard-muscle basis, and could so shake off their burden of flesh without interfering seriously with their business, they would be glad to try it. Let us see if this can be done.

In the summer of 1877 the writer met a gentleman of middle age, whom he had known for years, and who has been long connected with one of the United States departments in New York city. A very steady, hard-working officer, his occupation was a sedentary one. Remembering him as a man, till recently, of immense bulk, and being struck with his evident and great shrinkage, we inquired if he had been ill. He replied that he had not been ill, that for years he had not enjoyed better health. Questioning him as to his altered appearance, he said that, on the eighteenth day of January, 1877, he weighed three hundred and five pounds; that, having become so unwieldy, his flesh was a source of great hinderance and annoyance to him. Then he had determined, if possible, to get rid of some of it. Having to be at work all day, he could only effect his purpose in the evenings, or not at all. So, making no especial change in his diet, he took to walking, and soon began to average from three to five miles an evening, and at the best pace he could make. In the cold months he says that he often perspired so that small icicles would form on the ends of his hair. Asking if it did not come a little stiff sometimes, on stormy nights or when he was very tired, and whether he did not omit his exercise at such times, he said no, but, on the contrary, added two miles, which shows the timber the man was made of. On the eighteenth of June of the same year, just five months from the start, he weighed but two hundred and fifteen pounds, *having actually taken off ninety pounds*, and had so altered that his former clothes would not fit him at all. Since that time we have again seen him, and he says he is now down to two hundred, and that he has taken to horseback-riding, as he is fond of that. He looks to-day a large, strong, hearty man of about five feet ten, of rather phlegmatic temperament, but no one would ever think of him as a fat man.

Now here is a man well known to hundreds of the lawyers of the New York Bar, a living example of what a little energy and determination will accomplish for a person who sets about his task as if he meant to perform it.

During the war, M——, a member of the Boston Police force, known to the writer, was said to weigh three hundred and fifteen pounds, and was certainly an enormously large man. He went South, served for some time as stoker on a gunboat, and an intimate friend of his informed us that he had reduced his weight to one hundred and eighty-four.

A girl of fifteen or sixteen, and inclined to be fleshy, found that, by a good deal of horseback-riding daily, she lost twenty-five pounds in one year—so a physician familiar with her case informed us.

Brisk walking, and being on the feet much of the day—as Americans, for instance, find it necessary to do when they try to see the Parisian galleries and many other of Europe's attractions all in a very few weeks—will tell decidedly on the weight of fleshy people, and dispose them to move more quickly. When you can do it, this is perhaps not such a bad way to reduce yourself.

Now, if so many have found that vigorous muscular exercise, taken daily and assiduously, accomplished the desired end for them, does it not look as if a similar course, combined with a little strength of purpose, would bring similar benefit to others? In any case, such a course has this advantage: begun easily, and followed up with gradually increasing vigor, it will be sure to tone up and strengthen one, and add to the spring and quickness of movement, whether it reduces one's flesh or not. But it is a sort of work where free perspiration must be encouraged, not hindered, for this is plainly a prominent element in effecting the desired purpose.

But, while many of us know instances where fat people have, by exercise, been reduced to a normal weight, is it possible for a thin person to become stouter? A thin person may have a large frame or a slender one. Is there any work which will increase the weight of each, and bring desirable roundness and plumpness of trunk and limb?

Take, first, the slim man. Follow him for a day, or even an hour, and you will usually find that, while often active—indeed, too active—still he does no work which a person of his height need be really strong to do. Put him beside such a person who is not merely large, but really strong and in equally good condition, and correspondingly skilful, and let the two train for an athletic feat of some sort—row together, for instance, or some other work where each must carry other weight in addition to his own. The first mile they can go well together, and one will do about as much as the other. But as the second wears along, the good strength begins to tell; and the slim man, while, perhaps, sustaining his form pretty well, and going through the motions, is not quite doing the work, and his friend is gradually drawing away from him. At the third mile the disparity grows very marked, and the stronger fellow has it all his own way, while at the end he also finds that he has not taken as much out of him as his slender rival. He has had more to carry, both in his boat's greater weight, and especially in his own, but his carrying power was more than enough to make up for the difference. Measure the slim man where you will, about his arm or shoulders, chest or thigh or calf, and the other outmeasures him; the only girth where he is up, and perhaps ahead, is that of his head—for thin fellows often have big heads. The muscles of the stronger youth are larger as well as stronger.

Now, take the slim fellow, and set him to making so many efforts a day with any given muscle or muscles, say those of his upper left arm, for instance. Put some reward before him which he would like greatly to have— say a hundred thousand dollars—if in one year from date he will increase the girth of that same upper left arm two honest inches. Now, watch him, if he has any spirit and stuff, as thin fellows very often have, and see what he does. Insist, too, that whatever he does shall in no way interfere with his business or regular duties, whatever they may be, but that he must find other time for it. And what will he do? Why, he will leave no stone unturned to find just what work uses the muscles in question, and at that work he will go, with a resolution which no obstacle will balk. He is simply showing the truth of Emerson's broad rule, that "in all human action those faculties will be strong which are used;" and of Maclaren's, "Where the activity is, there will be the development."

The new work flushes the muscles in question with far more blood than before, while the wear and tear being greater, the call for new material corresponds, and more and more hearty food is eaten and assimilated. The quarter-inch or more of gain the first fortnight often becomes the whole inch in less than two months, and long before the year is out the coveted two inches have come. And, in acquiring them, his whole left arm and shoulder have had correspondingly new strength added, quite going past his right, though it was the larger at first, if meanwhile he has practically let it alone.

There are some men, either at the college or city gymnasiums, every year, who are practically getting to themselves such an increase in the strength and size of some particular muscles.

We knew one at college who, on entering, stood hardly five feet four, weighed but about one hundred and fifteen pounds, and was small and rather spare. For four years he worked with great steadiness in the gymnasium, afoot and on the water, and he graduated a five-foot-eight man, splendidly built, and weighing a hundred and sixty-eight pounds—every pound a good one, for he was one of the best bow-oarsmen his university ever saw.

Another, tall and very slender, but with a large head and a very bright mind, was an habitual fault-finder at everything on the table, no matter if it was fit for a prince. A friend got him, for awhile, into a little athletic work—walking, running, and sparring—until he could trot three miles fairly, and till one day he walked forty-five—pretty well used up, to be sure, but he walked it. Well, his appetite went up like a rocket. Where the daintiest food would not tempt him before, he would now promptly hide a beefsteak weighing a clean pound at a meal, and that no matter if cooked in some roadside eating-house, where nothing was neat or tidy, and flies abounded almost as they did once in Egypt in Pharaoh's day. His friends frequently spoke of his improved temper, and how much easier it was to get on with him. But after a while his efforts slackened, and his poor stomach returned to its old vices, at least in part. Had he kept at what was doing so much for him, it would have continued to prove a many-sided blessing.

If steady and vigorous use of one set of muscles gradually increases their size, why should not a similar allowance, distributed to each, do the same for all? See (Appendix V.) what it did in four months and twelve days for Maclaren's pupil of nineteen, whose upper arm not only gained a whole inch and a half (think how that would add to the beauty alone of many a woman's arm, to say nothing of its strength), and whose chest enlarged five inches and a quarter, *but whose weight went up eight pounds*! Or what it did (see Appendix IV.) for Sargent's pupil of nineteen, who in just one year, besides making an inch and a half of upper arm, and three and a half of chest, went up from a hundred and forty-five pounds to a hundred and sixty, or *a clean gain of fifteen pounds*. Or (see Appendix VI.) for Maclaren's man, fully twenty-eight years old, who, in seven months and nineteen days, made *sixteen pounds*; or (Appendix VII.) for his youth of sixteen, who in just one year increased his weight *full twenty-one pounds*!

These facts certainly show pretty clearly whether sensible bodily exercise, taken regularly, and aimed at the weak spots, will not tell, and tell pretty rapidly, on the thin man wanting to stouten, and tell, too, in the way he wants.

It will make one eat heartily, it will make him sleep hard and long. Every ounce of the food is now digested, and the long sleep is just what he needed. Indeed, if, after a hearty dinner, a man would daily take a nap, and later in the day enough hard work to make sure of being thoroughly tired when bedtime came, he would doubtless find the flesh coming in a way to which he was a stranger. Many thin persons do not rest enough. They are constantly on the go, and the lack of phlegm in their make-up rather increases this activity, though they do not necessarily accomplish more than those who take care to sit and lie still more.

The writer, at nineteen, spent four weeks on a farm behind the Catskills, in Delaware County, New York. It was harvest-time, and, full of athletic ardor, and eager to return to college the better for the visit, we took a hand with the men. All the farm-hands were uniformly on the field at six o'clock in the morning, and it would average nearly or quite eight at night before the last load was snugly housed away in the mow. It was sharp, hard work all day long, with a tough, wiry, square-loined fellow in the leading swath all the morning. But to follow him we were bound to or drop, while the pitchfork or rake never rested from noon till sunset. Breakfast was served at five-thirty; dinner at eleven; supper at four; and a generous bowl of bread-and-milk—or two bowls, if you wanted them—at nine o'clock, just before bedtime, with plenty of spring-water between meals; while the fare itself was good and substantial, just what you would find on any well-to-do farmer's table. And such an appetite, and such sleep! Solomon must have tried some similar adventure when he wrote that "the sleep of the laboring man is sweet, whether he eat little or much." Well, when we returned to college and got on the scales again, the one hundred and forty-three pounds at starting had somehow become a hundred and fifty-six! And with them such a grip, and such a splendid feeling! We have rowed many a race since, but there was as hard work done by some of that little squad on that old mountain farm as any man in our boat ever did, and there was not much attention paid to any one's training rules either.

It is notorious, among those used to training for athletic contests, that thin men, if judiciously held in, and not allowed to do too much work, generally "train up," or gain decidedly in weight, almost as much, in fact, as the fleshy ones lose.

Now, were the object simply to train up as much as possible, unusual care could be taken to insure careful and deliberate eating, with a generous share of the fat and flesh making sorts of food, and quiet rest always for awhile after each meal, to aid the digestive organs at their work. Slow, deep, abdominal breathing is a great ally to this latter process; indeed, works direct benefit to many of the vital organs, and so to the whole man. All the sleep the man can possibly take at night would also tell in the right way. So would everything that would tend to prevent fret and worry, or which would cultivate the ability to bear them philosophically. But most thin people do not keep still enough, do not take matters leisurely, and do not rest enough; while, if their work is muscular, they do too much daily in proportion to their strength.

They are very likely also to be inerect, with flat, thin chests, and contracted stomach and abdomen. Now the habit of constantly keeping erect, whether sitting, standing, or walking, combined with this same deep, abdominal breathing, soon tends to expand not only the lower ribs and lower part of the lungs, but the waist as well, so giving the digestive organs more room and freer play. Like the lungs, or any other organ, they do their work best when in no way constrained. Better yet, if the person will also habituate himself, no matter what he is at, whether in motion or sitting still, to not only breathing the lower half of the lungs full, but the whole lungs as well, and at each inspiration hold the air in his chest as long as he comfortably can, he will speedily find a quickened and more vigorous circulation, which will be shown, for instance, by the veins in his hands becoming larger, and the hands themselves growing warmer if the air be cold; he will also feel a mild and agreeable exhilaration such as he has seldom before experienced. Some of these are little things, and for that reason they are the easier to do; but in this business, as in many others, little things often turn the scale. Of two brothers, equally thin, equally over-active, as much alike as possible—if one early formed these simple habits of slow and thorough mastication, deep and full breathing, resting awhile after meals, carrying his body uniformly erect, and sleeping plentifully, and his brother all the while cared for none of these things, it is highly probable that these little attentions would, in a few years, tell very decidedly in favor of him who practised them, and gradually bring to him that greater breadth, depth, and serenity, and the accompanying greater weight of the broad, full, and hearty man.

And what about the old people? Take a person of sixty. You don't want him to turn gymnast, surely. No; not to turn gymnast, but to set aside a small portion of each day for taking such body as he or she now has, and making the best of it.

But how can that be done? and is it practicable at all for a person sixty years old, or more? Well, let us see what one, not merely sixty, but eighty, and more too, had to say on this point. Shortly after the death of the late William Cullen Bryant, the New York *Evening Post*, of which he had long been editor, published in its semi-weekly issue of June 14th, 1878, the following letter:

"MR. BRYANT'S MODE OF LIFE.

"The following letter, written by Mr. Bryant several years ago, describing the habits of his life, to which he partly ascribed the wonderful preservation of his physical and mental vigor, will be read with interest now:

"'New York, March 30, 1871.
"'*To Joseph H. Richards, Esq.:*

"'MY DEAR SIR,—I promised some time since to give you some account of my habits of life, so far at least as regards diet, exercise, and occupations. I am not sure that it will be of any use to you, although the system which I have for many years observed seems to answer my purpose very well. I have reached a pretty advanced period of life, *without the usual infirmities of old age*, and with my strength, activity, and bodily faculties generally, in pretty good preservation. How far this may be the effect of my way of life, adopted long ago and steadily adhered to, is perhaps uncertain.

'I rise early; at this time of the year about half-past five; in summer, half an hour or even an hour earlier. Immediately, with very little encumbrance of clothing, I begin a series of exercises, for the most part designed to expand the chest, and at the same time call into action all the muscles and articulations of the body. These are performed with dumb-bells, the very lightest, covered with flannel, with a pole, a horizontal bar, and a light chair swung around my head. After a full hour, and sometimes more, passed in this manner, I bathe from head to foot. When at my place in the country, I sometimes shorten my exercises in the chamber, and, going out, occupy myself for half an hour or more in some work which requires brisk exercise. After my bath, if breakfast be not ready, I sit down to my studies till I am called.

"'After breakfast I occupy myself for awhile with my studies, and then, when in town, I walk down to the office of the *Evening Post, nearly three miles distant,* and, after about three hours, return, always walking, *whatever be the weather or the state of the streets.* In the country, I am engaged in my literary tasks till a feeling of weariness drives me out into the open air, and I go upon my farm or into the garden and prune the fruit-trees, or perform some other work about them which they need, and then go back to my books. I *do not often drive out, preferring to walk.*

m, sir, truly yours,
"'W.C. BRYANT.'"

The same paper also contained the following:

"REMINISCENCES OF A FORMER BUSINESS ASSOCIATE.

"Mr. William G. Boggs, who knew Mr. Bryant intimately for many years, has given the following reminiscences to a representative of the *Evening Post*:

"'During the *forty years that I have known him, Mr. Bryant has never been ill—never been confined to his bed, except on the occasion of his last accident. His health has always been good.*

"'Mr. Bryant was a great walker. In earlier years he would think nothing of walking to Paterson Falls and back, with Alfred Pell and James Lawson, after office hours. *He always walked from his home to his place of business, even in his eighty-fourth year.* At first he wouldn't ride in the elevator. He would never wait for it, if it was not ready for the ascent immediately on his arrival in the building. Of gymnastic exercises he was very fond. Every morning, for half an hour, he would go through a series of evolutions on the backs of two chairs placed side by side. He would hang on the door of his bedroom, pulling himself up and down an indefinite number of times. He would skirmish around the apartment after all fashions, and once he told me even *"under the table."* Breakfast followed, then a walk down town; and then *he was in the best of spirits* for the writing of his editorial article for that day.

"'He was a constant student. His daily leading editorial constituted, and was for many years, the *Evening Post*. Sometimes he would not get it written until one o'clock. "Can't I have it earlier?" I asked him one day. "Why not write it the evening before?" "Ah," he replied, "if I should empty out the keg in that way, it would soon be exhausted." He wanted his evenings for study. "Well, then, can't you get down earlier in the morning?" He said, "Oh yes." A few months afterward he exclaimed, with reference to the change: "I like it. *I go through my gymnastics, walk all the way down,* and when I get here I feel like work. I like it."'"

Mr. Boggs also tells us that Mr. Bryant's sight and hearing were scarcely impaired even up to his death.

How remarkable these facts seem! Here a man, known to the whole civilized world, says at seventy-seven that he "has reached a pretty advanced period of life without the usual infirmities of old age, and with his strength, activity, and bodily faculties generally in pretty good preservation." Wouldn't most of us like to do that? Are there not men who would promptly give millions, not "for an inch of time," but to be able to reach seventy-seven, and to say of themselves what Mr. Bryant could say of himself at that age? Nor at seventy-seven only, but at eighty-four, for his friend tells the same thing of him then.

And notice what he did: "Every morning," not for two or three minutes only, but "for half an hour, he would go through a series of evolutions on the backs of two chairs placed side by side." The "dips" which have been recommended in another place,[K] and which are so excellent for making the chest strong and keeping it so, are doubtless the "evolutions" meant; and as the great majority of men, whether young or old, have not strength of triceps and pectorals enough to even struggle through one of them, some conception can be formed of how wonderfully wiry and strong this large-headed, spare-bodied, illustrious old man was, to say nothing of the strength of purpose which would keep him so rigidly up to his work at an age when most men would have thought it their unquestionable duty to coddle themselves. Just think of a man over eighty "pulling himself up and down"—evidently on the "horizontal bar" he mentions—"an indefinite number of times!" Or "always walking" down to the office of the *Evening Post*, nearly three miles distant, and, after three hours, return, always walking, whatever be the weather or the state of the streets! Or of never waiting for the elevator if it was not ready, but always walking up the *nine flights* from the street to his office! And the writer has often seen him going up the top flight, and, instead of his step being faltering and feeble, it was uniformly *a trot!*

See what two other old men did—in some ways even a more remarkable thing than Mr. Bryant's great activity. The following despatch is from the *New York Herald* of February 23d, 1879:

"THE OLD MEN'S WALK.

"New Haven, Conn., Feb. 22, 1879.

"The walk between Thomas Carey, of the New York Cotton Exchange, and Joseph Y. Marsh, of this city, terminated to-night at a quarter of an hour before the appointed time, Marsh withdrawing. Carey had walked 211 miles and a fraction, to 209 miles and a corresponding fraction for Marsh. After the walk Marsh said that he was convinced that he had been beaten, and Carey made a speech expressing satisfaction with the manner in which he had been treated. The walk began on Wednesday of the present week, at eleven o'clock, and terminated at forty-five minutes past ten to-night. Carey is a great-grandfather, and is sixty-four years old, and Marsh sixty-three. Both had trained for the walk. It is understood that they will walk again in New York."

Sixty miles a day for three days and a half, and by a great-grandfather at that! Any man, or any horse, might well hold that a good day's work.

This activity among men so far on in years seems surprising. And why? Because, as people get past middle life, often from becoming engrossed in business, and out of the way of anything to induce them to continue their muscular activity, oftener from increasing caution, and fear that some effort, formerly easy, may now prove hazardous to them, they purposely avoid even ordinary exercise—riding when they might, and indeed ought to, walk, and, instead of walking their six miles a day, and looking after their arms and chests besides, as Bryant did, gradually come to do nothing each day worthy of the name of exercise. Then the joints grow dry and stiff, and snap and crack as they work. The old ease of action is gone, and disinclination takes its place. The man makes up his mind that he is growing old and stiff—often before he is sixty—and that there is no help for that stiffness.

Well, letting the machinery alone works a good deal the same whether it is made of iron and steel, and driven by steam, or of flesh and blood and bones, and driven by the human heart. Maclaren cleverly compares this stiffening of the joints to the working of hinges, which, when "left unused and unoiled for any length of time, grate and creak, and move stiffly. The hinges of the human body do just the same thing, and from the same cause; and they not only require frequent oiling to enable them to move easily, but they *are* oiled every time they are put in motion, *and when they are put in motion only*. The membrane which secretes this oil, and pours it forth over the opposing surfaces of the bones and the overlying ligaments, is stimulated to activity only by the motion of the joint itself." Had Bryant spared himself as most men do, would he have been such a springy, easy walker, and so strong and handy at eighty-four? Does it not look as if the half-hour at the dumb-bells, and chairs, and horizontal bar, and the twelve or fifteen thousand steps which he took each day, had much to do with this spring and activity in such a green old age? Does it not look almost as if he had, half a century ago, read something not unlike the following from Maclaren:

"The first course of the system may be freely and almost unconditionally recommended to men throughout what may be called middle life, care being taken to use a bell and bar well within the physical capacity. The best time for this practice is in the early morning, immediately after the bath, and, when regularly taken, it need not extend over more than a few minutes."

Whether Bryant had ever seen these rules or not, the bell, the bar, and the morning-time for exercise make a noticeable coincidence.

Looking at the benefit daily exercise brought in the instances mentioned, would it not be well for every man who begins to feel his age to at once adopt some equally moderate and sensible course of daily exercise, and to enter on it with a good share of his own former energy and vigor? He does not need to live in the country to effect it, nor in the city. He can readily secure the few bits of apparatus suggested elsewhere[L] for his own home, wherever that home is, and so take care of his arms and chest. For foot-work there is always the road. Is it not worth while to make the effort? He can begin very mildly, and yet in a month reach quite a creditable degree of activity, and then keep that up. And if, as Mr. Bryant did, he should last till well past eighty, and, like him, keep free from deafness and dimness of vision, from stiffness and shortness of breath, from gout, rheumatism, paralysis, and other senile ailments, as he put it himself, "without the usual infirmities of old age"— indeed, with his "strength, activity, and bodily faculties generally in pretty good preservation," and all that time could attend promptly to all the daily duties of an active business as he did, as Vanderbilt did, as Palmerston did, as Thiers did—is not the effort truly worth the making? And who knows what he can do till he tries?

CHAPTER XI.

HALF-TRAINED FIREMEN AND POLICE.

THERE are two classes of men in our cities and larger towns who, more than almost any others, need daily and systematic bodily exercise, in order to make them efficient for their duties, and something like what men in their lines ought to be. In times of peace they do in many ways what the army does for the whole country in war-time—they protect life and property. These are the police and firemen.

The work of some of the firemen before they reach a fire is even more dangerous than when actually among the flames. The examining physician of one of our largest life insurance companies told the writer that he frequently had to reject firemen applying for insurance, because they had seriously injured their hearts by running hard to fires when quite untrained and unfit for such sudden and severe strain on the heart and lungs, imposed, as it usually is, under much excitement. The introduction of steam fire-engines has in part done away with this, though even they often have a man to run before and clear the way; but in smaller places, of course, the old danger exists. Thorough and efficient as this steam-service is in many ways, and trained as the men are to their duties, they are, very many of them, not nearly so effective as they might easily be, and as, considering the fact that the fireman's work is their sole occupation, they ought to be. Men of pluck and daring, and naturally strong, often for days together they have no fire to go to, and so sit and stand around the engine-house for hours and hours. Soon they begin to fatten, until often they weigh thirty or forty pounds more than they would in good condition for enduring work. Having no daily exercise which gives all parts of the body increased life and strength, neither the stout nor thin ones begin to be so strong, so quick of movement, or enduring as they would be if kept in good condition. To carry from an upper story of a high building a person in a swoon or half suffocated, and to get such a burden safely down a long narrow ladder through stifling smoke and terrible flame, is a feat requiring, beside great nerve and courage, decided strength and endurance. Exposure during long periods, perhaps drenched through, perhaps holding up a heavy hose in the winter's cold, or in many another duty all firemen well know, often without food or drink for many hours, taxes very severely even the strongest man.

And what training have these men for this trying work outside of what the fire itself actually gives? Practically, none. Suppose every man on the force was required to spend an hour, or even half an hour, daily in work which would call into play not all their muscles, but simply those likely to be most needed when the real work came. Suppose each of them a wiry, hard-muscled, very enduring man, good any day for a three or five mile run at a respectable pace, and without detriment to himself, or to go, if need be, hand over hand up the entire length of one of their long ladders—to be, in short, as strong, as handy, as enduring, as even a second-rate athlete. Is there any question that a force made up of such men would be far better qualified for their work, and far more efficient at it, than the firemen of any of our cities are now?

And if they think they at present have considerable daily exercise, so does a British soldier decidedly more, in his daily drilling, and the whole round of his duties; and yet, after Maclaren had one of them exercising for but a brief period, but in a way to bring up his general strength, the soldier said, "I feel twice the man I did for anything a man could be set to do." Would it hurt a fireman or a policeman any to have that feeling? Would the latter not be more inclined to rely on his own strength, and less on his club?

If the training suggested seems too hard, look at the younger men in blacksmithing, for instance, and many other kinds of iron-work, swinging, as they often do, a heavy sledge for the whole day together; at the postmen, walking from morning to evening, often up many flights of stairs, and all the year round, and in all weathers; at the iron-puddler, the hod-carrier, the 'longshoreman—all at work nearly or quite as hard, not for one short hour only, but through all the burden and heat of the day. Many of these men are not nearly as well paid as the firemen, and none of them begin to have as great responsibility, or are at any moment likely to be called on to take their lives in their hands, and perhaps to save other lives as well.

Let us look at the policeman. What exercise has he? Standing around, and considerable slow walking, for six hours out of each twelve. Is there anything to make him swift of foot? No. Anything to build up his arms and expand his chest, to make those arms help him in his business, and those hands twice as skilful for his purposes as before? Very little. Taught to use his hands he is, but never empty; there must be something in them—a club or a revolver. And so comes what legitimate result? Why is it that in a conflict, or even a threatened one—or, too often, not even then—and when the culprit, while drunk, is wholly unresisting, we constantly hear of these dangerous weapons being drawn and freely used? Some of the very men set to preserve the peace are themselves every now and then making assaults wholly uncalled for, always cowardly, and often brutal, and such as an athletic man, proud of his strength, would have scorned the idea of making, but, instead, would have so quickly displayed his skill and strength that the average offender, especially when he recalled the fact that the officer had the law on his side, would have soon ceased resisting. Every intelligent New Yorker will at one recognize that there is far too frequently good ground for such editorial comment, grim as is its satire, as the following from a well-known New York journal, of September 20th, 1878:

"A COMPLICATED POLICE CASE.

"We have recorded from time to time in the T—— various interesting police cases. With all our skill and experience, however, we could not prevent a shade of monotony stealing over them. When in nine cases out of ten the picture presented is that of a policeman clubbing a man nearly to death, by what resource of rhetoric can you avoid monotony? For the sake of variety, as well as for the public good, many people wish that a citizen would occasionally kill a brutal policeman; only that, in thus ridding the world of a human brute not worthy to live in it, the mockery that is called justice in New York and Brooklyn would probably also send out of the world the inoffensive citizen who had accomplished the good work. In a recent case, however, matters have become most ingeniously complicated. One policeman has arrested another. On Tuesday night two men got into a fight in the Bowery. Detective Archibald, who was in plain clothes, undertook, it is said, to arrest them. Then, it is stated, Officer Lefferts arrived, and arrested the whole party, detective and all. We say that this is a complicated case; but so it did not seem to Justice Morgan, of the Jefferson Market Police Court. If a policeman arrests a citizen, it is no longer possible for the latter to get justice. He is glad if he can get away with a whole skull and unbroken ribs. But one policeman arresting another! The only way in which this can be set right depends upon which policeman had the most influence at head-quarters."

And what sort of man is he who is thus too free with his weapon? Take him in New York city, for instance. Out of nearly twenty-five hundred policemen, it is entirely safe to say that one-third—and it would probably be much nearer the truth to say that all of two-thirds—are unathletic men, and that a very large proportion of these are either clumsy, unwieldy, and short-winded, or not possessed of even average bodily strength. Even in their uniforms this is quickly apparent; but the true way to judge is to see them stripped, either in gymnastic costume or at the swimming-bath. Any number of them have indifferent legs; there are any number of stout, paunchy fellows; and old ones, too, doubling over with their years; flat-chested ones, big-footed and half-built men.

Try to select some of these men for a physical feat, say of speed and endurance, like running or rowing, and see how few would be fit for the work. Pair them off, give them gloves, and set them to boxing, and there would scarce be one hundred good sparrers out of the whole brigade. Once, right in front of Trinity church-yard, on Broadway, we saw two of the Broadway squad put up their hands for a little good-natured sparring, and the way they did it would hardly have been creditable to a ten-year-old. To see two great, hulking six-footers, ignorant of the first rudiments of good sparring, actually whirling their fists round and round each other as if winding yarn, and with no sort of idea how to use even one hand, let alone two, was positively ridiculous. A hundred-pound thief, handy with his fists and quick of foot, could have slapped their faces, and, if they could run no better than they sparred, could have been at the Battery before either of them was half-way. And what good would their weapons have been? Their revolvers they would hardly dare to use in a crowded street at broad noon, nor would they have been justified in so doing. And their clubs—of what use would they be if the culprit was a block away?

The writer once saw a fellow, apparently a sneak-thief, cutting across the City Hall Park, in front of the *Tribune* building, at a clipping pace, while some distance behind came one of those majestic but logy guardians of the peace, making about one foot to the other's two, and, finally, seeing how hopeless was the pursuit, bringing his club around and throwing it after the escaping thief—and with what result? Excellent for the thief, for, instead of coming anywhere near him, it passed dangerously close to the abdomen of a worthy but obese citizen, who chanced to be passing that way.

At a public exhibition, held early in 1878, under the auspices of these very Metropolitan Police, at the Hippodrome, in New York, where doubtless the very best boxers on the whole force were on the boards, and with ten thousand spectators to spur them on to their utmost, the thoroughly skilful and accomplished workmen could be counted almost on the thumbs; while, in the tug of war, the string of policemen were overhauled and pulled completely down by the Scottish Americans, who weighed half a hundred weight less per man than their uniformed antagonists; though it is but just to add that, later on, the latter did manage to win, yet what was that to brag of?

The same Police Department held a regatta on the Harlem River on the twenty-ninth of August, 1878, for which there were many entries; yet out of them all with one or two exceptions, there was no performance which was not of the most commonplace character, unworthy of an average freshman crew, and this though many of the rowers were burly, heavy men. One of the single-scullers actually did not know how to back his boat over some fifty feet of water, and, after four ineffectual endeavors, had to be told how to do so from the referee's boat.

Now place the whole force abreast on a broad common, or in half a dozen lines, and set them to run a mile at no racing pace; at no such gait even as John Ennis went in March, 1879, when, after 474 miles of walking and running in one single week, he ran his 475th mile in six minutes eleven seconds, but let them go at even a horse-car pace; and if five hundred get over even half the distance it will be a surprise, while of those who do, many stand a good chance to feel the effects for days, if not for life. We asked the best known police captain in New York city, the president of the old Police Athletic Club, whether he thought one-half of the whole twenty-five hundred could run a mile at any pace which could actually be called a run. After deliberating a little, he said he did not think they could. One of the most successful athletes on the force, in reply to the same question, said: "I'll bet my neck against a purse that not one-third of them can do it." Another, a magnificent-looking man, standing over six feet three in height, and weighing upward of two hundred and fifty, not only strongly inclined to the same opinion, but, when urged to tell how successful he himself would probably be in such a trial, he gave, with a little sudden color in his cheeks, substantially as follows, this most interesting incident from his own experience:

Standing in a rear room on the main floor of the station-house of the —— Precinct, he heard a scream. Going quickly to the street, a lady told him that she had been robbed of her pocket-book, while a young person gliding gracefully, and, as the sequel proved, quite fleetly, around the corner, lent force to the statement. Away went the engine of the law, his mighty form bending to the work, with his best foot foremost. Turning up one of the broad avenues, the one hundred and twenty-five feet or so of the thief's start had now shrunk to seventy-five, and, as the two sped on at a grand pace,

> "All and each that passed that way
> Enjoyed the swift 'pursuit.'"

Block after block was passed, but the gap would not close. Go as he would, do his mightiest and his best, it was of no use; that lawless young man would somehow all the time manage to keep just seventy-five feet to the fore. Four blocks are now done, and so is the policeman; and bringing up all-standing— blown, gasping, exhausted—he cannot even muster breath enough to shout, but, reaching his big hand out in front of him, and looking at the young person gently fleeting, with seemingly unabated vigor, into the dim distance, he sadly points to him, for that is all he is just now equal to. Fortunately for the interests of justice and good order, that point is well taken, for a brother officer sees it, and, rising to the occasion, dashes off after the misguided young person up the avenue. "Life is earnest" now, surely, for the latter. Still he has nearly a hundred feet start, and maybe this second guardian of the peace will not stay any better than did his illustrious predecessor. So down to it he settles again, and the street enjoys the fun. Block after block slips away, and so does the official wind, for, at the end of four blocks more, no perceptible decrease of the gap having yet been made, patrolman number two "shuts up." Yes, literally, for he too cannot even yell, but, like the first, striking a tragic position, he points to the flying culprit. And is justice to be cheated out of her victim after all, even now, when she a second time is sure that she has reached the point? And is this light-fingered and light-heeled young person to escape the minions of the law—and all this in broad daylight too, and right on Sixth Avenue? So it certainly seems. But stop! Justice, after all, is to prevail, for lo! a third pursuer has now caught the trail, and is off like a fast mail-train. Have a care now, young man! No brass buttons adorn your pursuer this time; but the self-appointed private citizen, now in your wake, runs as the wicked flee. There is no cart-horse pace about his work; but with one clean, business-like spurt, he swoops down on the now disturbed young man, and, clutching his upper garments, holds him neatly until the reserves come up, and then hands him over for his six months on the island."

One more illustration may suffice. The *New York Herald* of December 20th, 1878, referring to a burglary which had been committed in the 28th Precinct, said that suspicion fastened on a young man known as "Sleepy Dick." Detective Wilson got on the supposed offender's trail, and the nearer he got to him the worse grew his character for strength, daring, and ferocity. At last he came up with "Sleepy Dick" on Second Avenue yesterday.

"'The jig's up, Sleepy,' said the detective; 'you're wanted.'

"'What for?' calmly inquired the other, straightening upon the coal-box.

"'Cracking a crib.'

"'How long a stretch?'

"'A fiver, sure.'

"'I'm not your meat then, cully,' and Dick bolted for the corner with no sleepiness about him. Wilson grabbed him firmly by the collar, though, and there was a scene of plunging and tearing witnessed by the crowd around them that eclipsed Cornwall or Græco-Roman wrestling.

"Suddenly a revolver came flashing out of Wilson's pocket.

"'I'm taking this pot,' said he, coolly.

"'Show your hand,' growled 'Sleepy.'

"'A straight flush;' and Wilson levelled the pistol at his head.

"'That takes this pile,' Dick sullenly assented, and he moved on quietly as far as Sixty-first Street. Once at the corner, he plunged backward and broke loose. The detective's revolver came down on his head with a thud, but he rallied under the blow, sprung aside, and made for the river. He was fleet of foot, and, as he flew down the street, he kept looking over his shoulder, evidently in fear of a passing bullet. But the detective was coming on after him, bound to run him down, and as they passed First Avenue the hue and cry was taken up by two other policemen, who joined in the pursuit. There was fully a block between 'Sleepy' and his pursuers when he neared the river. He saw his advantage, turned into a stone-yard, dodged among the bowlders, scaled a fence, and made off. Dick has been in the hands of the police before this week, but managed to get away."

Is there no lesson for our city rulers in such facts as these? If our police are men of only four block power; if they are so blown in that little distance that they are utterly helpless, and all they can do is, one after another to point to the escaping felon and indulge in these "brilliant flashes of silence," inwardly imploring some good civilian to kindly catch that thief; if a youngster can first indulge in a tough wrestle with a detective, and then, taking a heavy blow on his head from the butt of a revolver, not only empty-handed get away from his would-be captor, but, although the latter is joined by two policemen, soon put a whole block between him and them, and springing over a fence, go, after all, "unwhipt of justice," does it not strike the reader that a little improvement in the speed and stay of our policemen might do no harm? Had it not better be conceded that it is hopeless for many of the Broadway squad, for instance, in their present condition, to attempt to catch a thief by running; after him, and would it not be well to provide each of them with a lasso, for short-range work, and initiate them in its uses at once? In this way they could certainly make sure of one of those light-heeled gentry once in a while, perhaps—for example, one fond of lady's ear-rings. And who believes that officers always report their failures to catch thieves, or that the public ever hears of one-half of such cases?

Let us see, too, where this physical incapacity may lead to graver consequences than the mere allowing a detected thief to run at large. In the great cities there have sprung up within a few years back storehouses for the safe-keeping of securities, plate, important papers, and other valuables. Hedged around with plates of steel, chronometer-locks, massive bolts, and several watchmen, and connected with the nearest police station by wires so arranged that the doors cannot be opened without sounding the alarm at the station-house, the public naturally put their trust in them, and their property too. Within recent years we also hear far more than formerly of burglars going not in pairs or threes, but in gangs of half a dozen or more, and of cracking safes always thought impenetrable. Now, suppose that a descent were made on the largest one of these safe depositories in America, the one under the New York Stock Exchange, and by a dozen first-class cracksmen. Their business hours are generally between one and four in the morning. That they work with wonderful sagacity, daring, and despatch, is attested by such brilliant performance as that at the Northampton Bank robbery, or when they in a little time, one morning, relieved the Manhattan Bank of a few millions, and that right within a block of police head-quarters in New York city. Suppose that, by collusion or otherwise, the robbers get through the outer door. Unlike the Bank of England, there is no platoon of soldiers on guard. They silence the three or four who oppose them. They come to the inner doors, the opening of which alarms the police. At the station-house, when that alarm sounds, three or four, or maybe more, more or less drowsy officers start and run for the Stock Exchange, some eight hundred feet away. Is there any especial reason why they should be any less exhausted when they get there than the two policemen who failed to catch the Sixth Avenue thief, or the two who let another on First Avenue run clear out of their sight? The four blocks the former two policemen ran do not make much over eight hundred feet. Suppose that three or four, not half-grown fellows like "sleepy" Dick, but stalwart desperadoes, used to rough work, quietly await the arrival of these worthy, but well-blown patrolmen. How long would it take the thieves to at least check the advance, if not also considerably impair the usefulness of men so nearly gone that they could not speak, and whose hands shook so that aiming a revolver effectively would be practically out of the question?

And might not the Press justly have some pretty plain comment to make, then, on the physical inefficiency of our police force, and wonder why it had not been insisted on long ago that they be trained as men have to be in other callings, until they are fit for their work? Hear Dr. Morgan, in "University Oars," on fat and unwieldy men, and their unfitness for emergencies calling for strong and quick work: "When, therefore, we hear of a man who, at twenty years of age, weighed 12 stone (168 pounds), and in after-life inclining to corpulency, has reached the abnormal weight of 17 or 18 stone (238 or 252 pounds), we must not consider him proportionately stronger: on the contrary, he should rather excite our pity and commiseration—the *five or six stone distributed over his body being composed wholly of adipose tissue.* He is thus as completely enveloped in blubber as though he were a whale or a seal. His muscles being heavily weighted, *his powers of locomotion are necessarily limited*; and, handicapped in this manner, it is no easy task for him to drag his unwieldy frame on some sweltering 12th of August over the trying inequalities of a Highland moor."

The broken-winded man, or a man out of wind, is almost as useless in an emergency calling for sharp and sudden work as a broken-winded horse. The standing around of the policeman, heavily shod and heavily clad, and the lazy, aimless walking, will never make him hardy, tough, and difficult to face, or likely not to use his club where a strong, quick man would never need it. Swollen hands and feet, and soft, flabby flesh will be the result; and for the variety of sudden and dangerous work which he may be called upon to do at any moment he is not half fitted; and if he trains no more for his work than he does now, he never will be.

Again, in the matter of looks—not the least important, by any means, of the qualifications of a police-officer—are they all that they might be, and that they really ought to be?

When a thousand of them, averaging two hundred pounds apiece, parade down Broadway, with brass buttons gleaming, and every belt well filled, it is easy enough for Press or citizen to say, "What a fine-looking body of men!" But now, notice them closely, and most of them are inerect, many are round-shouldered, and few are at once thoroughly well-built men and in good condition, being either loose-jointed, too fat, or too thin. Contrast their marching and bearing with that of the little West Point battalion on parade, every man erect, clean-cut, precise, wiry, and athletic; light and young, to be sure, but most hardy, quick, and manly. Now, we know what it is to be erect. We soon discover that the bulk, the sunburn, and the uniforms have gone far toward making the favorable impression, which ought to have been better based, and that almost every one of these policemen is plainly faulty.

Now, suppose every one of these twenty-five hundred men, besides being, as most of them already are, both courageous and faithful in the performance of duty, was a skilful and hard-hitting boxer, a good, steady, long-distance runner, a fair wrestler, a strong swimmer, a sound, hale, thoroughly well-made man. Let the vicious classes once know—and how long would it take them to learn?—that in a race between them and the policeman the latter would be pretty sure to win; let it be known that, when he once caught his man, the odds would be decidedly in his favor, and that that man would not get away; let every member of the force be justly known as a formidable man to face, and one whom the offender had better avoid—and what an advance it would be in both the moral and physical efficiency of the force! Now let the riot come, and see what that little band of twenty-five hundred trained men could do against ten times their number. To-day they have nothing which makes them enduring at quick, hard work, and that is what is wanted for mobs. If they had an abundance of that which would make them so, the plying of a locust for an hour or two among a lot of unorganized roughs would be almost a diversion, and a game they could continue at by the week if need be.

And why should not every city in our land have, instead of men very many of them too often far out of condition, these same well-trained men, educated, as men have to be in nearly every other calling, directly for their work, and all dexterous and able? Is it asking too much? The preparation necessary to it will not compare in its exhausting effects with what the war-policeman—the soldier, who is not paid a quarter as much—must do without a murmur: the long forced marching, weighted like a pack-horse, the broken sleep, the stinted food, the bad shoes, the long absence from home, and the lack of all comforts. Why not insist on a regime which, if the fat man could go through and retain his corporosity, would make him welcome to retain it; if the thin man could be up to every day's work in it, then he could stand far more than he looked equal to? But if either failed, out with him. There need be no fear that good substitutes could not be had in abundance.

93

This is no question of mere health, and symmetry of make, and reasonable strength, as with the ordinary citizen. It is a matter of fitness for ordinary duties—duties often of very great importance to the public weal, which may spring up at any moment, and which call for unusual physical resources. It is a matter of substituting for dangerous weapons, rashly wielded, and when that wielding is often wholly uncalled for, men who, in any ordinary street-brawl, need no weapon, and would scarcely think of using one, any more than would a Morrissey, a Heenan, or a Hyer.

As nearly as possible in the centre of each four precincts in the larger cities hire a hall, say about eighty feet by forty, and the higher the better, well lighted and ventilated, and easily heated. Two hundred dollars, carefully spent, would buy all needed apparatus, and as much more would keep it swept and dusted, lighted and warmed. Twenty-five cents a month from each of four hundred policemen would be twelve hundred dollars a year, which would cover, beside these items, rent and salary of teacher as well. For the teacher need be with them but a little while daily; for, in about all the exercises necessary to make men good ordinary runners and boxers, a teacher up to his work can drill the men in squads. What they want is not intricate and technical knowledge, but plain, straightforward, swift, hard work, and plenty of it, and the condition which keeps them easily up to it. Or, better yet, put these gymnasiums in charge of the department, if equally rigid economy could be insured. Then require each man to spend fifteen minutes there every other day, sparring—after he had the rudiments—with some companion who can give him all the exercise he wants, and on the alternate days let an equal period of time be spent in running, not at racing pace, but still good lively work of the kind which brings good lungs and good legs. Now, at the annual or semi-annual athletic meeting, let picked men from each precinct contend in foot-races, both for short and long distances; and, to give their work an even more practical turn, give some sneak-thief a reasonable start in such contests, and let the officers, in full uniform of course, catch him if they can. Now the waistbands will begin to lessen, and a considerably smaller measure of cloth will cover the man, but it will clothe a man who, unarmed and unaided, can whip almost half a dozen such flabby, untrained, unskilful fellows as he used to be. For every duty which may at any moment become his, whether light or heavy, mild or violent, he will be far better qualified in almost every respect than before, yet no better in his line than any good business man requires each person in his employ to be in his, no matter what their particular duties may be.

CHAPTER XII.
SPECIAL EXERCISE FOR ANY GIVEN MUSCLES.

WHILE symmetrical and thorough physical development are not at all common among Americans, and undeveloped, inerect, and weak bodies almost outnumber any other kind, the general want of familiarity with what will develop any given muscles, and bring them up to the fulness and strength which ought to be theirs, is even more surprising. If proof is wanted of this, let the reader ask himself what special work he would choose to develop any given part; the muscles of the forearm, for instance, or those of the front of the chest. If he has ever paid any attention to his physical development—and thousands and tens of thousands have not—he may know one or two things which will bring about the desired result; but even if he has attended the gymnasium a good deal, he will often be surprised to find that his time there was mainly spent in accomplishing some particular feat or amount of work, rather than in bringing about the special development of any given part, or general development of the whole body.

Now, while the exercises which bring any given set of muscles into play are very numerous, if a few can be grouped together which shall be at once simple and plain, and shall call either for inexpensive apparatus or none at all, which will also enable almost any one, by a little energy and determination, to bring up any limb or muscles now weak, they may prove of value.

To develop the Leg below the Knee.

The main part of the leg below the knee, for instance, is composed of muscles which raise the heel. Stand erect, with the head high, chest out, and shoulders down, keeping the knees all the time well sprung back, having the feet about three inches apart, with the toes turned slightly outward. Now slowly raise the heels until they are high off the floor, and the whole weight rests on the soles and toes. Now drop slowly down. Then repeat. Next place the hand on the muscles of the calf, and while at first not firm, feel them harden as you rise, and all doubt as to whether the exercise in question uses these muscles will speedily vanish. Continue this exercise at the same rate, keeping at it until you have risen fifty times. Now, it will not be necessary, with most persons, to have to place the hand on these muscles to learn if they are brought into play, for already that is becoming very plain in another way, one that is bringing most conclusive proof to the mind—internal evidence it might well be called. Unless the calves are unusually strong, long before the one hundredth effort there is an unmistakable ache in them, which, in the majority of instances, will cause the person to stop outright from sheer inability to proceed. It has not taken much time to get a pretty thorough measure of about what power there is in one set of muscles at least. All doubts are gone from his mind now as to whether one exercise he knows will call into play the muscles of his leg below the knee or not. It is equally plain that it is not his forearm, or upper arm, or the back or front of his chest which has been in action, for none of these have felt fatigue, the tire being all confined to the muscles in question.

Again, had there been beside him two men of nearly the same weight, but one of small and feeble calves, the other having them shapely and well-developed, is there any doubt which of the two could have kept at the exercise the longer, yet with the less fatigue? Few men need be told that a muscle, unused to work at first, can gradually, by direct and systematic exercise, be strengthened; but not a few there are who are unaware that with the new strength comes increased size as well.

Yet, to those familiar with athletic work, it is as plain as that you must have your eyes open if you want to see. A gentleman of our acquaintance, of magnificent muscular and vital development, was not satisfied with the girth of his calves, which was 14¼ inches. At our suggestion he began practising this simple raising and lowering of the heels. In less than four months he had increased the girth of each calf one whole inch. When asked how many strokes a day he averaged, he said, "From fifteen hundred to two thousand;" varied some days by his holding in each hand during the process a twelve-pound dumb-bell, and then only doing one thousand or thereabouts. The time he found most convenient was in the morning on rising, and just before retiring at night. Instead of the work taking much time, seventy a minute was found a good ordinary rate, so that fifteen minutes at each end of the day was all he needed. But this was a great and very rapid increase, especially for a man of thirty-five; far more than most persons would naturally be contented with, yet suggestive of the stuff and perseverance of the man who accomplished it.

Here, then, one of the most effective exercises which could be desired for the strengthening of these muscles is accomplished actually without apparatus, without one cent of expense—one which can be practised anywhere, in the largest or the smallest room, in-doors or out, on land or while at sea.

But there are many other exercises which will bring this same development. Now stand erect again, with head and chest high, shoulders low, and knees sprung back. Start off at an ordinary pace, and walk. But, instead of, as usual, putting the foot down and lifting it without thinking about it, this time, just as it leaves the ground, press hard with the soles and toes. Go on for a block or two, and you will suddenly find that your calves are having new and unwonted duties—indeed, a very generous share of work. Keep on for a mile—if you can. Good a walker as you thought yourself before, a mile of this sort will be a mile to be remembered—certainly for a few days, till the ache gets out of your calves.

If walking with this new push is not hard enough on flat ground, try it up-hill. It will not be long before these muscles will ache till it will seem as if you must have a whole gymnasium concealed in them somewhere.

Another exercise for the same muscles, which can also be learned in a moment, and a little of which will suffice at first, is running on the toes, or, rather, on the soles and toes. Here the whole weight is held by, and pushed from, first the muscles of one calf, then of the other. One will not go far at this without convincing proof of the value of this work to the parts in question.

Of two brothers of our acquaintance—one a boy of thirteen, the other a little fellow of four—the former walks with no especial spring, and performs his running flat-footed. But the little fellow, whether walking, standing, or running, is forever on his toes, and with his knees sprung well back. The former has rather slim legs and no great calf; the latter beautifully developed calves, round, full, and symmetrical, noticeably large for a boy of his size and age.

Again, work, harder, and telling more directly on the calves, and hence calculated to increase their size and strength faster even than any of these, is hopping on one foot—a really grand exercise, and one of the speediest for bringing strong legs and a springy step. There is not the relief in it that there is in walking or running. There the rest is nearly twice as long as here. Here the work is almost continuous, and soon tires the strongest muscles. Jumping also exercises these muscles powerfully, and, practised steadily, soon brings them up. Well developed and strong, these muscles are of great value in dancing, adding astonishingly to the ease and grace so valued in this accomplishment, and to endurance as well. Horseback-riding, where the foot is pushed but a little way into the stirrup, and the whole weight thus thrown on the toes; rowing, especially with the sliding seat, where the feet press hard against the stretcher; leaping; ordinary walking uphill, and walking on the toes alone— these all call these muscles into most vigorous play, and, when practised steadily and with energy, are among the most rapid means known for increasing, not the strength of the calves alone, but their girth as well.

Try a summer of mountain climbing. Look at the men who spend their lives at it. Notice the best stayers in the Alpine clubs, and almost invariably they are found to have large and powerful calves, especially where their knees are not bent much in stepping. In a personal sketch of Bendigo, the once celebrated British prize-fighter (now a quiet Christian man), much stress was laid on the fact that his calves measured a clean sixteen inches about. Yet, to show that gentlemen are sometimes quite as strong in given directions as prize-fighters, look at Professor Maclaren's own memorandum of not only what a splendid pair of legs he himself had at the start, but what a little mountain climbing did for them; for he says that in four months of Alpine walking, averaging nine hours a day, his calves went up from sixteen inches to seventeen and a quarter! and his thighs from twenty-three and a half inches to twenty-five. If instances nearer home are sought, and yet where neither anything like the time Maclaren took was given to it, nor any of the very severe work of the gentleman referred to a little earlier, look at what Dr. Sargent accomplished, not with one solitary man but with two hundred, at Bowdoin College; not giving nine hours a day to it, but only "half an hour a day, four times a week, for a period of six months." In this very brief time, and by moderate exercises, he increased the average girth of the calf of these whole two hundred men from twelve and a half inches to thirteen and a quarter. There was one pupil, working four hours a week instead of four half-hours, and for one year instead of six months, who increased his calves from thirteen and a half inches to fifteen—an actual gain of a quarter of an inch more in two hundred and eight hours of exercise, much of which was given to other muscles, and did not tell on the calves, than Maclaren made in nine hundred hours of work, most of which kept these muscles in very active play.

In all exercises for these muscles, indeed in all foot-work, shoes should be worn with soles broad enough to prevent the slightest cramping of the foot, and so giving every part of it its natural play.

There remains one other prominent muscle below the knee, that in front, running down along the outer side of the shin-bone. Develop the calf fully, as is often done, and omit this little muscle and the work which calls it into play, and there is something wanting, something the lack of which causes a lack of symmetry. Fast walking, when one is unused to it, especially when the knees are held pretty straight, will work this muscle so vigorously as to make it sore. But a plain, safe, and simple exercise for it, yet one which, if protracted, will soon swell it into notice, and give it unwonted strength and beauty, is effected by stooping down as low as possible, the feet being but a few inches apart, and the heels never being allowed to rise even a quarter of an inch off the floor. Lift the heels, and this muscle is at once relieved.

Laying any weight on the foot, and lifting it clear from the ground, will also call on this muscle. So will fastening the feet into straps, like those on a boat-stretcher or rowing-weight, and swaying the body of the sitter back and forth; for these muscles have heavy work to do to aid in pulling the body forward, so that the rower may reach his hands out over his toes for a new stroke. Simply standing on one foot, first holding the other clear of the floor, and then drawing it up as near as possible to the front of its own ankle, and then opening it as wide as you can, will be found a safe and reasonably effective way of bringing forward this small but useful muscle; while walking on the heels, with the toes drawn up high, is simpler yet. For those who want to run heavy risks, and are not contented with any exercise which does not threaten their necks, hanging by the toes from a horizontal or trapeze bar will be found to just fill the bill.

Work for the Front of the Thigh.

The muscles of the front thigh have a most intimate connection with those already mentioned, and, for ordinary purposes, a fair development of them is more necessary than of those below the knee. In common walking, for instance, while the calf gets something to do, the thigh gets far more, especially when the step is low and flat, and the heel never raised far from the ground. A man will often have large and strong thighs, and yet but indifferent calves. A prominent Harvard oarsman, a strong and fast walker, and a man of magnificent development in most points, was once examined carefully by Greenough, the sculptor. "I should know you were an American," said he, "because you have no calves;" and, indeed, his mistake in developing splendid arms, and trunk, and thighs, and forgetting all about the calves, is far too common a one among our athletes to-day; though the prominence they are beginning to give to running helps mend matters in this respect.

Scarcely any muscles are easier brought into action than these of the upper or front thigh. Stand erect, with head and chest high, and the feet about six inches apart. Now, bend the knees a little, say until the head has dropped vertically six inches. Then rise to the perpendicular again. Repeat a few times, and it will not be long till these muscles will be felt to be in lively action, and this exercise prolonged will make them ache. But this movement is very much akin to that in dancing, the latter being the harder of the two, because the weight is first on one foot, then on the other, while in the former it is always on both.

Again, instead of stooping for a few inches only, start as before, with head and neck rigidly erect, and now stoop all the way down; then rise again. Continue this movement several times, and generally at first a few repetitions will be found to be quite enough. By-and-by, as the strength increases, so should the number; and, if time is to be saved and the work condensed, keep dumb-bells, say of a tenth of your own weight, in the hands during the operation.

A more severe tax yet is had by holding one foot far out, either in front or back, and then stooping down wholly on the other foot. Few can do this many times, and most persons cannot do it at all. For swiftly bringing up a thigh at present weaker than its mate, and so restoring the symmetry which should always have been there, this work is almost unparalleled.

Jumping itself, either high or flat, is admirable for the thighs. Charles Astor Bristed, in his "Five Years in an English University," says that he at one time took to jumping, and was astounded at the rapid progress he made in a branch of athletics at which before he had been no good. Maclaren says that hardly any work will quicker bring up the whole legs; but this will probably prove truer where a large number of moderate jumps are taken daily, than where a few extreme efforts are made.

Both fast walking and running bring vigorous action to these muscles; slow walking does little for them, hence the number of weak, undeveloped thighs among men who do little or no quick foot-work. A man, too, whose body is light and thin, may do a deal of fast walking without greatly enlarging his thighs, because they have comparatively little to carry. But let him, after first getting thoroughly used to fast and continued walking, carry weight awhile, say a twenty-five-pound bag of shot or sand, or a small boy, on his back, or dumb-bells in his hands—of course, on a gymnasium track, or some other course where his action will be understood—and he will find that the new work will soon tell, as would, also, long-distance running, even though not weighted, as Rowell so eminently shows.

Good, stiff long-distance walking is excellent for the front thigh; but running is better, especially when done as it ought to be, namely, not flat-footed, but with the heel never touching the ground. Any sort of running or walking, at any pace protracted enough to bring moderately tired muscles, will tell, especially on these in question; while severe work over a long distance will give them a great task, and the consequent ability and size. Many a man may do a little desultory running daily, perhaps for a week or two together once a year, and not find his thighs enlarge or toughen materially. But let him put in a few minutes each day, for several months together, at steady smart running, as far as he can, and go comfortably, and now, besides the work becoming easy, comes the desired size and strength as well. The hopping, which was so good for the calves, is hardly less so for these muscles, and is one of the best possible movements to develop them in the shortest time.

Dancing, long continued, also tells here, as an acquaintance of ours found, who used to lead the German frequently at Newport; for, though far from being an athlete, he said that he daily ran a mile during the season, just to keep his legs in good order for the duties his position demanded.

A more moderate exercise than the running, though not always so available, is walking uphill. This, besides, as already mentioned, doing so much for the calves, tells directly and markedly on the thighs as well. Skating makes a pleasant substitute for walking during a part of the colder months, and, when much distance is covered daily, brings strong and shapely thighs.

The farmer and the laboring man, in all their heavier work done stooping over their tasks—such as lifting, shovelling, picking, and mowing—use the thighs much, but keep them so long fixed in one position, with little or no varying exercise to supple and limber them and the joints, that both gradually stiffen, and their instep soon begins to lack elasticity, which tendency is too often increased by heavy, stiff, and unwieldy boots.

Swinging forward when rowing, either in a boat or at the toe-straps, after first swinging far back, takes these upper muscles in a way quite the reverse of their ordinary use, they now aiding to pull the whole trunk forward, and so acting like two long hooks.

All lifting of heavy objects from the ground, standing in almost any position, tells heavily on these muscles, being about the severest momentary test they can have, greater even than in jumping. But occasional heavy lifting tends rather to harden the muscle than to rapidly increase its size, protracted effort at lighter but good-sized weights doing the latter to better advantage.

Brisk horseback-riding keeps these muscles very actively employed. Every sort of work which calls for frequent stooping down does the same. Persons who take short steps, and many of them, if they walk with vigor, are likely to have legs thicker and stouter everywhere than they who stride out far, but make the whole step as easy for themselves as possible.

Hardly any of the muscles are so useful and valuable as these. One may have weak arms and trunk, yet with strong thighs he can walk a long distance daily, and not be nearly so fatigued as those much stronger elsewhere and weaker here, and, as many men have little or no other exercise than walking, they are often contented with fair development here, and practically none of any account elsewhere. It is astonishing, too, to notice how a man accustomed for years to a poor shambling sort of a gait will, with strict attention to taking a clean and strong step over a certain distance daily, with a determination to take no other sort of gait, soon improve the strength and shape of his thighs.

As hopping on one foot is a swift way to develop the calf, so frequent stooping down as low as possible and rising again, daily, at first without weights, but eventually with them, is the sure way to speedily enlarge and strengthen the thighs.

To Enlarge the Under Thigh.

The muscles of the under thigh do not get nearly so much to do as those in front, in many persons seeming almost not to exist. A bad walk, with the knees always slightly bent, is partly accountable for this; and a man accustomed to such a walk, and trying suddenly to walk erect, with his knees firmly knit, and bowed slightly back, soon tires and aches at the operation, which, to one in the habit of walking erect, long ago became natural.

The exercise already recommended, of pressing the sole of the foot hard on the ground just as it leaves it, is scarcely more beneficial to the muscles of the calf than to these; likewise walking uphill, that telling finely on them. Standing, as does the West Pointer in his setting-up drill, and, with knees unbent, trying to touch the floor with the hands, tells in this region. Fastening a weight of any sort, a dumb-bell or flat-iron, to the ankle, say with strap or towel, and raising the foot as high up backward and outward as possible, and repeating till tired; putting the foot in the handle of the pulling-weight, and frequently drawing it far down; or, standing with back to the wall, and placing the heel against the base-board of the room, or any solid vertical surface, and pressing hard many times—these all tell on this hidden under muscle, which, small as it is, is a most essential one, and especially in looks, while running with the foot thrown high behind, excels them all.

To Strengthen the Sides of the Waist.

But while the legs have been so actively engaged, there are other parts which have not been idle, so that the same work brings other strength as well. In every step taken, and especially every vigorous one, as in fast walking or in running, the muscles at the sides of the waist have been all the time at work, a prominent duty of theirs being to aid in holding the body erect.

Notice a man weak just here, and see his body sway a little from side to side as he walks, seeming to give at the waist. Were such a one to practise daily hopping straight ahead, on one foot, and then on the other, until he could by-and-by so cover half a mile without fatigue, he would find his swaying propensity fast disappearing; and if he has been troubled with a feeble or unshapely waist, that also will have gradually changed, until at the end it has become firm and well-set.

Take the long balancing-pole of the tight-rope walker, and try to walk a rope awhile, or try the more simple expedient of walking on the railroad rail, and these muscles are at once uncommonly busy. Notice the professional tight-rope man, and see how strong he is here, especially when to the weight of his own body he adds another, as did Farini when he carried a man on his shoulders across the Niagara River; or as the Eastern porter, with his huge weight of luggage; or the carrier at the meat-market, who shoulders a whole side or more of beef and marches off with it. These men soon get great and unusual power in these side muscles. Wrestling also, whether Cornish or Græco-Roman, or indeed almost any sort, tells directly and severely here. If one prefers to use apparatus made specially, the opposite cut shows a simple device of Dr. Sargent's, which he made purposely to bring up and strengthen these muscles.

Standing in front of it, with head and neck erect and chest out, and grasping the ends of the bar A A', the operator simply turns it, first well up to the right, then to the left, and then repeats the movements until he has enough. As he turns, the rubber straps B B stretch more and more, of course getting stiffer the farther the bar is turned. It would scarcely be possible to hit upon a better appliance for improving these valuable side muscles, and yet without fear of overdoing them.

Fig. 5.

The Abdominal Muscles.

Nor do these include all the muscles which the foot-work arouses to action. Take the horizontal bands or layers of muscle across the abdomen. Every step forward moves them, and the higher and more energetic the step, the more they have to do. A man who is not strong in these muscles will usually have a feeble walk, and very often will double forward a little, until he is in about the position of the two hands of a clock at two minutes past six, giving him the appearance of being weak here. But the strong, high step tilts the body slightly back, and gives these muscles so much to do that they soon grow good at it, and shapely and powerful accordingly.

Another advantage comes from having these muscles strong, and from forming the habit of stepping as he does who has them so. By walking thus erect, the shoulders, instead of pressing over on the chest as the man tires, and so cramping his breathing, are so habitually held back that it is easier to keep them there, and the consequent fuller respiration keeps him longer fresh. This is very conspicuous in the case of one of the most famous pedestrians in the world to-day, its ex-champion long-distance walker, Daniel O'Leary. Take him when in good condition, and in one of his long tramps; on the first mile or the four hundredth, it is always the same: there he is, with head up, shoulders well back, and working busily, and—the most noticeable thing—the whole centre of the body, from the waist to the knees, thrown, if anything, actually forward of a vertical line, instead of as far, or often much farther, back of it; indeed, the point farthest forward is about two inches below his belt. A fair though not clear idea of what is meant can be had from the following sketch of him, taken at the time, on the latter part of his five-hundred-mile walk with Hughes, "the Lepper," on the track in the Hippodrome, in New York city, during the first week of October, 1878. Hughes, while proving himself a very tough and determined man, showed, as is too often the case with professional athletes, great ignorance of many things which would have helped him much had he known and followed them, and none more, perhaps, than this very matter of correct position.

O'Leary's freshness, no matter how many hundred miles he has just walked, is remarkable. This rational way of carrying the body during a difficult feat, besides giving the heart and lungs full room for vigorous action, also gives the stomach and other vital organs ample play; for a glance at the sketch shows none of the thinness of flank and general sunken-in look at the waist in O'Leary so plain in Hughes, and so common among walkers in the later miles of the race.

Fig. 6.

Singularly enough, a little boy, only eleven years old, and but three feet nine inches high, has copied, or rather acquired—for it seems he had never seen this sensible step and carriage of O'Leary—with astonishing success, as witness the following sketch of his performance from the *New York Herald* of October 11th, 1878. Foolish in the extreme as it is to allow such half-grown youngsters to attempt such feats, it is doubtful if the annals of the cinder-path can match such prodigious stay and skill in one so young:

"AN EMBRYO O'LEARY

"Between the Grand Central Depot and Madison Avenue and Forty-second and Forty-fourth streets is a vacant square, which the boys of the neighborhood have been utilizing as a race-track. Every day dozens of them may be seen scurrying round the track, intent on making the best time ever known. Yesterday afternoon a five-mile walk was in progress, which was headed by a very small boy, who at once attracted the attention of the by-standers by his peculiarly rapid and easy gait. He kept ahead of the other contestants, and finally distanced them by two laps, and won in the time of 48m. 2s.

"After this race, at the request of the lookers-on, he travelled around the track once (which is one-seventh of a mile) in 1m. and 15s. *He walks very erect, steps like O'Leary, and does not seem to be easily fatigued.* This time is still more surprising, considering that he is only eleven years old and but three feet nine inches high, so that he cannot take a very long step.

"In a conversation with him it was learned that his name was Joe Havey, residing at No. 144 East Forty-third Street. He has never seen a professional walk, so that his walking ideas are his own. With a little practice he bids fair to become a No. 1 pedestrian."

But there are other ways of bringing up these useful abdominal muscles, equally easy to learn.

Sit down at the rowing-weights, placing the feet in the toe-straps. Now sway the body back and forth, and, placing the hand on the muscles in question, feel how they harden. An ordinary bit of strap screwed to the baseboard of one's room, so that each foot shall have a loop of it to go into, and then a stool or cassock some eight inches high to sit on, save the expense of the rowing-weights, yet produce the desired result with these muscles.

Lie flat on the back, as, for instance, just on awaking. Taking first a deep, full breath, draw the feet upward, keeping the knees unbent, until the legs are vertical. Lower them slowly till horizontal, then raise again and continue. It will not take many minutes—or seconds—to bring these muscles enough work for one morning.

Or this time keep the legs down, and, first filling the chest, now draw the body up until you are sitting erect. Then drop slowly back, and repeat. This will be likely to take even less time than did the other, but it will tell tremendously on these muscles. Indeed, most people are so weak in them, that they can hardly do this once. Yet men who have them strong and well-trained will lie flat on their backs on the floor or gymnasium mat, and while some one holds their ankles, taking a two-hundred-pound man, lying across their chest at right angles with it, will raise him several times till they are in erect sitting posture.

Sitting on one of the parallel bars in the gymnasium, and placing both feet under the other, and now dropping the body back until it is horizontal, then rising to vertical and repeating, is very hard work for these abdominal muscles, and should only be practised by those already strong here.

These muscles are brought into direct and vigorous play in rowing, to such an extent that no man who has them weak can be a fast oarsman over any ordinary racing distance. Indeed, this is the very region where young rowers, otherwise strong, and seemingly fit for hard, fast work, give out first.

Every time the foot is raised in running, these muscles are called to active duty far more than in walking, and the high, strong, sharp step works them severely, so that no man weak here could be a fast runner with good action. Jumping, vaulting, leaping, all bring them into sudden, spasmodic, almost violent action. Let a man mow awhile, when unused to it, and see how soon it tells across this region, the muscles aching next day from the twisting motion.

The latest invention purposely for these muscles is also one of Sargent's, on the following plan: The pupil lies on the plank A A', or, rather, sits on it, when A' is a little back of vertical, so as, for instance, to form with A the angle A B A'. With feet in the toe-straps C C', he sways gently forward and back as long as he can without fatigue. From day to day, as these muscles gain strength, A' is dropped lower and lower, until finally it is on a level with A. Or a strap may be placed over the forehead and fastened to A', and, with the feet in the toe-straps, the person may lift his body up till vertical, drawing the weight E with him as he rises.

Counterwork for the Abdominal Muscles.

But nearly all the exercises just named for the abdominal muscles, while they make them strong and handsome, tend to contract rather than lengthen them; and for men of sedentary life inclined to stoop a little forward while sitting, some work is needed which shall stretch these muscles, and aid in restoring them to their natural length.

Stand erect. Now gradually draw the head and shoulders backward until as far past the vertical as possible. Return slowly to erect position. In the drawing back, these muscles were stretched to a greater length than usual, and in those who accustom themselves to drawing far back in this way, like the contortionists of the circus, these muscles grow wonderfully elastic, such men being able not only to touch their heads to their heels, but now and then to go farther yet, and drink water from a tumbler set between their feet.

Fig. 7.

But while there is no need of such extreme work, moderate performance in this way directly tends to stretch and lengthen muscles which, in the great majority of people, are somewhat cramped and shortened by habitual standing, sitting, or lying, with the back either flat or almost curved outward, instead of slightly hollowed in, and with the consequent sinking of the chest. All work above the head, such as swinging clubs, or an axe or sledge; putting up dumb-bells, especially when both hands go up together; swinging by the hands from rope or bar, or pulling the body up till the chin touches the hands; standing with back to the pulley-weights, and taking the handles in the hands, and, starting with them high over the head, then pushing the hands far out forward; standing two or more feet from the wall, and, placing the hands side by side against it about as high up as your shoulders, then throwing the chest as far forward as possible; the hauling down ropes by the sailor; the ceiling-work of the plasterer and the painter, and the like—these all do excellent service in bringing to these important muscles the length and elasticity they ought to have, and so contributing materially to the erect carriage of the body. All kinds of pushing with the hands, such as one does in putting them against any heavy substance and trying to push it before him, striking out in boxing, in fencing, or single-stick, with dumb-bells, or in swimming, are capital; while the drawing of the head and shoulders back swiftly, as in boxing to avoid a blow, can hardly be surpassed as an aid in this direction.

To enlarge and give Power to the Loins.

Before leaving the waist, there is one more set of muscles which demand attention; and if one has them weak, no matter how strong he may be elsewhere, he is weak in a place where he can ill afford to be, and that is in the loins, or the main muscles in the small of the back, running up and down at each side of the spine. In many of the heavier grades of manual labor these muscles have a large share of work to do. All stooping over, when lifting is done with a spade, or fork, or bar, whether the knees are held straight or bent, or lifting any weight directly in the hands, horizontal pulling on a pulley-weight, rope, or oar—in short, nearly every sort of work where the back is actively employed, keeps these muscles thoroughly active. You cannot bend over without using them. Weed awhile, and, unless already strong in the loins, they will ache.

A laboring man weak here would hardly be worth hiring. A rowing-man weak here could never be a first-rate oar till he had trained away the weakness. Heenan, with all his grand physique, his tremendous striking-power, his massive development above the waist, would not have made nearly as enduring an oar as the sturdier, barrel-chested Morrissey, or as the broad-loined Renforth did make. Strong loins are always desirable. He who has them, and is called on in any sudden emergency to lift any heavy weight, as the prostrate form of one who has fallen in a swoon, for instance, is far less likely to work himself serious, if not permanent, injury here than he who has them untrained and undeveloped.

Development above the Waist.

Little or no work has been suggested, so far, aimed purposely to develop any muscles above the waist. Indeed, it is no uncommon thing, especially among Englishmen, to find a man of very strong legs and waist, yet with but an indifferent chest and shoulders, and positively poor arms. Canon Kingsley had discovered this when he said to the British clergy, "I should be ashamed of being weak. I could not do half the little good I do here if it were not for that strength and activity which some consider coarse and degrading. Many clergymen would half kill themselves if they did what I do. And though they might walk about as much, they would neglect exercise of the arms and chest, and become dyspeptic or consumptive."

Let us look at a few things which would have proved useful to the brave canon's pupils. The connection between the arms and the muscles, both on the front and back of the chest, is so close that it is practically impossible to have arms thoroughly developed, and not have all the trunk muscles above the waist equally so. Fortunately, as in foot-work, the exercises to develop these muscles, without having to resort to expensive apparatus, or often to any at all, are very numerous.

With a pair of dumb-bells, at first weighing not over one-twenty-fifth of what he or she does who uses them, and gradually, as the strength increases, substituting larger ones, until they weigh, say, one-tenth of his or her weight, there is scarcely a muscle above the belt which cannot, by steady and systematic work of never over half an hour daily, be rounded and strengthened up to what it ought to be in a thoroughly developed, strong, and efficient person of its owner's sex, size, and age.

Filling out the Shoulders and Upper Back.

Notice now what these dumb-bells can do for the shoulders and upper back.

Stand erect again, with the chin up and chest high (in all these exercises stand erect where it is possible), and have the dumb-bells in the hands hanging easily at the sides. Now carry them slowly backward and upward, keeping the arms straight at the elbows, and parallel, until the hands are about as high as they can well go. Hold them there a moment, then drop them slowly to the sides. Do it again, and keep on until you begin to feel like stopping. Note the spot where you feel it, and you will find that the under or inner muscles of the part of the back-arm which is above the elbow, also those on the shoulder-blade, and the large muscles of the back directly under the arms, have been the ones in action. Laying one dumb-bell down, now repeat the above exercise with the remaining one, say in the right hand, this time placing the left hand on the back just under the right arm, or on the inner portion of the triceps or upper muscle of that right arm. These muscles will be found vigorously at work, and hardening more and more the higher the bell is carried or the longer it is held up.

A little of this work daily, begun with the lighter dumb-bells, and increased gradually by adding to the number of strokes, or taking larger bells, or both, and long before the year is out, if the person is steady and persevering at it, decided increase in the strength, size, and shapeliness of the upper back will follow.

What has been thus done with the dumb-bells could have been done nearly or quite as well with any other small, compact body of the same weight which could be easily grasped by the hands, such as a pair of window-weights, flat-irons, cobble-stones, or even chairs, whichever were convenient. Where there's a will there's a way; and if one really means to get these or any other muscles strong and handsome, the way is really surprisingly simple and easy.

Now, instead of using the dumb-bells, stand erect, facing the pulley-weights at the gymnasium, or at home if you have them, taking care only that they weigh at least what the dumb-bells would. Grasping the handles, draw them far back and up, the hands, in other words, doing precisely what they did with the bells, and the same results will follow.

Rowing, either at the oar or the rowing-weights, would have told equally hard on these muscles, and, as already pointed out, on many others besides, the weight of the body itself aiding the development as it would not with the bells or weights. It would also broaden the shoulders and spread them apart, more, perhaps, than almost any other known exercise. But, like any other single exercise calling certain muscles into play and leaving others idle, taken as substantially one's only exercise, as is too often the case with rowing-men, it brings a partial and one-sided development, making the parts used look too large for the rest, the fact being that the rest have not been brought up as fast as the former. Unless one's chest is unusually broad and strong, and often, even if it is, constant rowing warps his shoulders forward, and tends directly to make him a round-shouldered man,[M] while the upper arm, or that part above the elbow, has had practically no development, the inner part of the triceps or back-arm alone being called to severe duty, but the bulk being almost idle. Courtney, the greatest sculler the United States has yet produced —a large man, standing six feet and half an inch in height, strongly made in most parts, and weighing ordinarily nearly a hundred and ninety—is a good instance of how rowing does little for the upper arm; for while his forearm is almost massive, measuring exactly thirteen inches in girth, the upper arm, doubled up, barely reaches fourteen. A well-proportioned arm, of which the forearm girths thirteen, should measure above all fifteen and a quarter. Again, while Courtney's forearm feels sinewy and hard, the upper is not nearly so hard, and does not give the impression of having seen very stiff service. His chest, too, is not so large by over two inches as ought to go with a thirteen-inch forearm.

Beside these exercises with the dumb-bells, the weights, and the oar, all the vocations which cause one to stoop over much and lift—such as most of those of the farmer, the laborer, and of the artisan in the heavier kinds of work—tell on these same muscles of the upper back and the inner side of the triceps, too often bringing, as already pointed out, a far better back than front, and so injuring the form and carriage. Lifting heavy weights where one stands nearly erect, as when practising on the lifting-machine, pulls very heavily on the extreme upper muscles of the back, those sloping off downward from the back of the neck to the shoulders.

To obtain a good Biceps.

Starting with the dumb-bells down at the sides, as before, raise them slowly and steadily in front until they nearly touch the shoulder—technically, "curl" them—holding the head up, the neck rigidly erect, and the chest expanded to its very utmost. Now lower the bells slowly to the sides again, and repeat, and so continue. In a very few minutes, often less than three, you will want to stop. The biceps muscles, or those forming the front of the upper arms, are getting the work this time, and by applying to that of one arm in action the hand of the other, it is at once found that this muscle is growing quite hard.

If no dumb-bell or other convenient weight is at hand, place one hand in the other, and bear down hard with the upper hand, holding the chest stubbornly out. Lift away with the lower hand, and, when it reaches the shoulder, lower it slowly to the side, and then raise again, and so continue. This will be found a good thing to know when a person is travelling, or away from home, and cannot readily get at such apparatus as he has in his own room.

Now stand erect in front of and facing the pulley-weights, and at about arm's-length from them; draw the hand horizontally in until it is close to the shoulder; let the weight drop slowly back, and then draw it to you again, and so go on. This is splendid work for the biceps, and will soon begin to swell and strengthen it; and then either increased weight, or more strokes daily, is all that will be needed.

Fasten a stout hook in a beam overhead, and hang a pulley to it. Run a rope through this, at one end of which you can attach weights, and tie the other to the middle of a thick cane or other stick, taking care to have the rope of such a length in all, that when the weight is on the floor the stick is about a foot above your head.

Begin with, say, one of your dumb-bells of not over one-tenth of your own weight. Grasping the stick with both hands, with their palms toward you, draw it downward until level with your chin; then let it go back; repeat, and continue till you begin to tire. If the single bell seems too light, attach both bells. After a few days with these, fasten on a basket or coal-hod, and increase the load until, say at the month's end, it weighs over half of what you do. If you can take this up a number of times without ache or ill-feeling, you are strong enough to take hold of a fixed bar and attempt to haul yourself up, as Mr. Bryant did,[N] until your chin touches your hand. But without this preliminary work, such pulling up, frequently as it is attempted, is a foolish and hazardous experiment, throwing a great strain on muscles quite unused to such a task, namely, on these very biceps muscles.

If, on the other hand, one has these muscles already strong, and can with ease pull himself up six or eight times, he will find this stick and weight an excellent affair for training the biceps of one arm, until it gets strong enough to pull him up without the other arm at all. For this simple and valuable contrivance the public is also indebted to Dr. Sargent, who is a regular Edison in devising simple and sensible gymnastic appliances, which he freely gives to all without patenting them.

Mounting a ladder or a rope hand-over-hand; lifting any weight in front of you, whether a feather or a barrel of sugar; picking up anything from the floor; holding weights out in front, or at your side, at arm's-length; pulling downward on a rope, as in hauling up a sail; hammering—in short, anything which bends the elbow and draws the hand in toward the shoulder, takes the biceps muscle; and, if the work is vigorous and persisted in, this muscle will ere long become strong and well-shaped.

To bring up the Muscles on the Front and Side of the Shoulder.

For the muscles on the front and side of the shoulder, holding out weights at arm's-length, either at the side or in front, will be found just what is wanted, the arms being horizontal, or the hands being held rather higher than that, the elbows remaining unbent. Holding the mere weight of the hands, as in boxing, but keeping at it awhile, keeps these parts well occupied; while the sword, or foil, or single-stick, freely plied, or the axe or bat, tell directly here.

Forearm Work.

Very many of these exercises for the biceps and shoulder have also called on the forearm, while those mentioned for the inner triceps have done the same. Very prominent among the latter is rowing, much of it soon bringing a strong forearm, especially on the inner and under side. Anything which necessitates shutting the hand, or keeping it partly or wholly shut; such as holding anything heavy in it, driving, chopping, fencing, single-stick, pulling one's self up with one hand or both, batting, lacrosse, polo, twisting the dumb-bells around when at arm's-length, or a chair, or cane, or foil, or sword, or broom-handle, if the dumb-bells are not convenient, carrying a weight in the hand, using any of the heavier mechanical hand-tools—all these, and more of their sort, will enlarge and strengthen the forearm, and will do much also for the hand. Probably the hardest work for the forearm, and that calling for the greatest strength here, is lifting very heavy weights suspended from a stick, bar, or handles which the hands grasp.

Exercises for the Triceps Muscles.

One prominent part of the arm remains, or, rather, one which ought to be prominent, though in most persons, both men and women, it is not. In boys and girls it is even less so. We refer to the rest of the triceps, or the bulk of what remains of the upper arm after leaving out the biceps and the inner side of the triceps. When well developed, this is one of the handsomest parts of the arm. No arm will look slim which has this muscle fully developed.

To bring that development, push with the hands against almost any heavy or solid thing you want to. If these muscles are small and weak, push the dumb-bells up over your head as much as you can daily, till a month's work has given them a start. For two or three minutes each day during that month, stand facing the wall, and about two feet from it. Now fall against it, or, rather, put your hands on it, about three feet apart and as high as your ears, and let your body drop in toward the wall till your chest nearly touches it, your face being held up and back. Then push sharply back till your body is again erect, and continue the movement. This exercise is as admirable as it is cheap.

If the triceps muscles are tolerably strong in the start, or in any case at the end of the month in which the last two exercises have been practised, try now a harder thing. Place the hands on the floor, hold the body out at full length and rigid, or as nearly so as you can, and push, raising the body till the elbows are straight. Now bend the elbows and lower again, till the face nearly touches the floor, keeping the body all the time as stiff and straight as possible, and then rise on stiff elbows again, and so on. If this is not hard enough work for the ambitious aspirant for stout triceps, he can vary it by clapping his hands between the dips, just as his face is farthest from the floor, though in such case it is sometimes well to have a nose accustomed to facing difficulty.

So far, in this work for the back-arm the hands at first held merely the weight of the dumb-bells; then, as they pressed against the wall, they had to bear part of the weight of the body, but not a large part, as that rested mainly on the feet. In the pushing from the floor the hands bore still more of it, but yet the feet had quite a share. Now try something where the hands and arms carry the entire weight of the body. Get up on the parallel bars, or on the bars in your door-jambs,[O] or, if no bars are convenient, place two stout chairs back to back, and then draw them about eighteen or twenty inches apart, and, placing one hand on each, holding the arms straight, lift the feet off the floor. Now lower till the chin is level with the hands, or nearly so, and then rise till the arms are straight, and then dip again, and so on, the knees and feet of course never resting on anything. Now you have one of the best known exercises for bringing quick development and good strength to the triceps or back-arm. When by steady daily trial you have gradually increased the number until you can do twenty-five fair dips without great effort, you have strong triceps muscles, and, if you have two legs and a reasonably heavy body to lift, good-sized ones at that. Most of your friends cannot manage five dips respectably, many scarcely one. But, lest you should feel too elated over your twenty-five, bear in mind that one gentleman in New York has accomplished over eighty without stopping, and this though he weighs upward of one hundred and eighty pounds; and if a reasonably accurate idea of what sort of back-arms were necessary for this marvellous feat, it may be had by observing the cut on the cover of this book. With a forty-four inch chest, his upper arm measures thirteen and a half inches down (half an inch more than Heenan's), and sixteen up, though he is but five feet ten inches in height, while Heenan stood four inches taller. He says that as surely as the ability exists to make many dips, so surely will there be a large back-arm, and it was hard work that brought him his. Slim arms may push up heavy dumb-bells once or twice, but it takes thick ones for sustained effort at smaller, though good-sized ones.

To Strengthen and Develop the Hand.

Very many of the exercises so useful in strengthening the forearm were at the same time improving the grip of the hand. But an evil of so much gripping or drawing the hand together is that, unless there is an equal amount of work to open and flatten it, it tends to become hooked. Notice the rowing-man's hand, and the fingers nearly always, when at rest, are inclined to be doubled in, as if half clutching something; and very often, where they have seen years of rowing, their joints get so set that the fingers cannot be bent back nearly as far as other people's. Some of the pushing exercises mentioned above for the triceps tend to counteract this, notably that where the fingers or the flat of the hands are pressed against the wall. An admirable exercise in this direction is, when you practice the pushing up from the floor for the triceps, to only touch the floor with the ends of the fingers and thumbs, never letting the palm of the hand touch it at all. This will soon help to rectify many a hand now rather cramped and contracted, besides bringing new strength and shape to the fingers.

To make any particular finger strong, attach a strap to the bar referred to on page <u>235</u>, and placing that finger in the strap begin with raising a small weight from the floor until you have drawn your hand down to your chin; then from day to day gradually increase both the weight and the number, until, before a great while, you may find that you can raise an equivalent of your own weight. Now attach the strap to any stationary object as high above your head as you can comfortably reach, say a horizontal bar, and pull yourself up till your chin touches your hand. Some gymnasts can do this several times with the little finger.

Just where the thumb joins the palm, and between it and the forefinger on the back of the hand, is a muscle which, while at first usually small, can be developed and enlarged by any exercise which necessitates pinching the ends of the thumb and forefinger together, such as carrying a plate of metal or other thin but heavy substance between the finger and thumb. Harder work yet, calling on both this muscle and a number of others of the hand, consists in catching two two-inch beams running overhead, as in the ceiling of a cellar, and about a foot and a half or two feet apart, and walking along, sustaining the whole weight by the grip, first of one hand, then of the other. He who can do this has very unusual strength of fingers.

For improving the ordinary grip of the hand, simply taking a rubber ball in it, or a wad of any elastic material, and even of paper, and repeatedly squeezing it, will soon tell. Simpler yet is it to just practice opening and shutting the hand firmly many times. An athletic friend of ours says that the man of his whole acquaintance who has the strongest grip got it just by practising this exercise.

To Enlarge and Strengthen the Front of the Chest.

Every one of the exercises for the biceps tells also on the pectoral muscles, or those on the front of the upper part of the chest, for the two work so intimately together that he who has a large biceps is practically sure to have the adjoining pectoral correspondingly large.

But there is other work which tells on them besides biceps work. Whenever the hands push hard against anything, and so call the triceps muscles into action, these muscles at once combine with them. In the more severe triceps work, such as the dips, the strain across these chest-muscles is very great, for they are then a very important factor in helping to hold up the weight of the whole body. This fact suggests the folly of letting any one try so severe a thing as a dip, when his triceps and pectoral muscles have not been used to any such heavy work. Many a person who has rashly attempted this has had to pay for it with a pain for several days at the edge of the pectoral, where it meets the breastbone, until he concluded he must have broken something.

Working with the dumb-bells when the arms are extended at right angles with the body, like a cross, and raising them up and down for a foot or so, is one of the best things for the upper edge of the pectorals, or that part next to the collar-bone.

This brings us to a matter of great importance, and one often overlooked. Whoever knows many gymnasts, and has seen them, stripped or in exercising costume, must occasionally have observed that, while they had worked at exercises which brought up these pectoral muscles until they were almost huge, their chests under their muscles had somehow not advanced accordingly. Indeed, in more than one instance which has come under our observation, the man looked as though, should you scrape all these great muscles completely off, leaving the bare framework, he would have actually a small chest, much smaller than many a fellow who had not much muscle. There hangs to-day—or did some time since—on the wall of a well-known New York gymnasium, a portrait of a gymnast stripped above the waist, which shows an exact case in point. The face of such a man is often a weak one, lacking the strength of cheek-bone and jaw so usual in men of great vitality and sturdiness—like Morrissey, for instance—and there is a general look about it as if the man lacked vitality. Many a gymnast has this appearance, for he takes so much severe muscular work that it draws from his vitality, and gives him a stale and exhausted look, a very common one, for example, among men who remain too long in training for contest after contest of an athletic sort.

The getting up, then, of a large chest, and of large muscles on the chest, while often contemporary, and each aiding the other, are too frequently wholly different matters.

And how is the large chest to be had?

To Broaden and Deepen the Chest itself.

Anything which causes one to frequently fill his lungs to their utmost capacity, and then hold them full as long as he can, tends directly to open his ribs, stretch the intercostal muscles, and so expand the chest. Many kinds of vigorous muscular exercise do this when done correctly, for they cause the full breathing, and at the same time directly aid in opening the ribs. It will be observed that frequently throughout these hints about exercising, endeavor has been made to impress on the reader that, when exercising, he should hold the head and neck rigidly erect, and the chest as high as he can. A moment's thought will show why. He, for instance, who "curls" a heavy dumb-bell, but does it with his head and shoulders bent over—as many do—while giving his pectorals active work, is actually tending to cramp his chest instead of expanding it, the very weight of the dumb-bell all pulling in the wrong direction. Now, had he held himself rigidly erect, and, first expanding his chest to its utmost by inhaling all the air he possibly could, and holding it in during the effort—a most valuable practice, by-the-way, in all feats calling for a great effort—he would not only have helped to expand his chest, but would find, to his gratification, that he had hit upon a wrinkle which somehow made the task easier than it ever was before.

Holding the head and neck back of the vertical, say six inches, with the face pointing to the ceiling, and then working with the dumb-bells at arm's-length, as above referred to, is grand for the upper chest, tending to raise the depressed collar-bones and the whole upper ribs, and to make a person hitherto flat-chested now shapely and full; while the benefit to lungs perhaps formerly weak would be hard to over-estimate.

Steady and protracted running is a great auxiliary in enlarging the lung-room. So is plenty of sparring. So is the practice of drawing air slowly in at the nostrils until every air-cell of the lungs is absolutely full, then holding it long, and then expelling it slowly. Most public singers and speakers know the value of this and kindred practices in bringing, with increased diaphragmatic action, improved power and endurance of voice.

Spreading the parallel bars until they are nearly three feet apart, and doing such arm-work on them as you can, but with your body below and face downward, helps greatly in expanding the chest. So does swinging from the rings or bar overhead, or high parallels, and remaining on them as long as you can.

Dr. Sargent's ingenuity has provided a simple and excellent chest expander. He rigs two ordinary pulleys over blocks some feet above the head, and from five to six feet apart, as in Fig. 8, and attaching weights at the floor ends of the ropes, puts ordinary handles on the other ends, and has the ropes just long enough so that when the weights are on the floor the handles are about a foot above the head. Now stand between and directly under them, erect, with the chest as full as you can make it, and keeping the elbows straight, and grasping the handles draw your hands slowly downward out at arm's-length, say about two feet. Next, let the weights drop gradually back, repeat, and so go on. This is excellent for enlarging the whole chest, but especially for widening it. A better present to a consumptive person than one of these appliances could hardly be devised.

Fig. 8.

Again, to deepen the chest from front to back, he hangs two bars, B and C, as in Fig. 9, and attaches the weight at the other end, A, of the rope, the bar B, when at rest, being about a foot above the height of the head. Standing, not under B, but about a foot to one side of it, and facing it, grasp its ends with both hands, and keeping the arms and legs straight and stiff, and breathing the chest brimful, draw downward until the bar is about level with the waist. Let the weight run slowly back, repeat, and go on.

A great advantage of both these contrivances, besides their small cost and simplicity, is that, as in nearly everything Dr. Sargent has invented, you can graduate the weight to suit the present requirements of the person, however weak or strong he or she may be, and so avoid much risk of overdoing.

Fig. 9.

In the exercises above named it will be noticed that there has been a sufficient variety for any given muscles to bring them within the reach of all. After this, how far any one will go in any desired line of development is a matter he can best settle for himself. What allowance of work to take daily will be treated of in the next chapter.

CHAPTER XIII.
WHAT EXERCISE TO TAKE DAILY.

An endeavor has been made thus far to point out how wide-spread is the lack of general bodily exercise among classes whose vocations do not call the muscles into play, and, again, how local and circumscribed is that action even among those who are engaged in most kinds of manual labor. Various simple exercises have been described which, if followed steadily and persistently, will bring size, shape, and strength to any desired muscles. It may be well to group in one place a few movements which will enable any one to know at once about what amount and sort of work is to be taken daily. Special endeavor will be made to single out such movements as will call for no expensive apparatus. Indeed, most of these want no apparatus at all, and hence will be within the reach of all. As it has been urged that the school is the most suitable place to accustom children to the kind and amount of work they particularly need, a few exercises will first be suggested which any teacher can learn almost at once, but which yet, if faithfully taught to pupils, will soon be found to take so little time that, instead of interfering with other lessons, they will prove a positive aid. Though perhaps imperceptible at the outset, in a few years, with advancing development, the gain made will be found not only to be decided, but of the most gratifying character.

Daily Work for Children.

Suppose the teacher has a class of fifty. If the aisles of the school-room are, as they should be, at least two feet wide, let the children at about the middle of the morning, and again of the afternoon session, stand in these aisles in rows, so that each two of the children shall be about six feet apart. Let the first order be, that all heads and necks be held erect. Once these are placed in their right position, all other parts of their bodies at once fall into place. The simplest way to insure this is to direct that every head and neck be drawn horizontally back, with the chin held about an inch above the level, until they are an inch or two back of the vertical. Now raise the hands directly over the head, and as high as possible, until the thumbs touch, the palms of the hands facing to the front, and the elbows being kept straight. Now, without bending the elbows, bring the hands downward in front toward the feet as far as can comfortably be done, generally at first about as low as the knee, taking care to keep the knees themselves absolutely straight; indeed, if possible, bowed even back. Now return the hands high over the head, and then repeat, say six times. This number twice a day for the first week will prove enough; and it may be increased to twelve the second week, and maintained at that number thereafter, care being taken to assure two things: one, that the knees are never bent; the other that, after the first week, the hands are gradually brought lower down, until they touch the toes. Some persons, familiar with this exercise, can, with the knees perfectly firm and straight, lay the whole flat of the hands on the floor in front of their feet. But after the first week, reaching the floor with the finger-tips is enough for the end sought, which is, namely, to make the pupil stand straight on his feet, and to remove all tendency toward holding the knees slightly bent, and so causing that weak, shaky, and sprung look about the knees, so very common among persons of all ages, to give way to a proper and graceful position.

Let the pupils now stand erect, this time with backs not bent forward, but with the body absolutely vertical. Raise the hands above the head as before, elbows straight, till the thumbs touch. Now, never bending body or knees a hair's-breadth, and keeping the elbows unbent, bring the hands slowly down, not in front this time, but at the sides just above the knees, the little finger and the inner edge of the hand alone touching the leg, and the palms facing straight in front. Now notice how difficult it is to warp the shoulders forward even an inch. The chest is out, the head and neck are erect, the shoulders are held low, the back vertical and hollowed in a little, and the knees straight. Carry the hands slowly back through the same line till again high over the head. Then bring them down to the sides again, and do six of these movements twice each day the first week, and twelve afterward.

While exercises aimed at any given muscles have been mentioned elsewhere, any one might follow them all up until every muscle was shapely and strong, and still carry himself awkwardly, and even in a slouchy and slovenly manner. This last-named exercise is directly intended to obviate this. If steadily practised, it is one of the very best known exercises, as it not only gives strength, but a fine, erect carriage. The whole frame is so held that every vital organ has free scope and play-room, and their healthier and more vigorous action is directly encouraged. This is one part, indeed the chief exercise, in the West Pointer's "setting-up drill;" and all who have ever seen the cadets at the Point will at once recall how admirably they succeed in acquiring and retaining a handsome carriage and manly mien.

To vary the work a little, and to bring special development to particular muscles, now let the pupil stand with arms either hanging easily at the sides, or else held akimbo, the head and neck always erect, with the heels about four inches apart, and the toes turned outward. Raise the heels slowly off the floor, the soles and toes remaining firm on the floor, sustaining the entire weight. When the heels are as high as possible, hold them there a moment; then lower slowly till the whole foot is on the floor again; then rise as before, and so repeat twelve times twice a day the first week, and then twenty-five for the following week, continuing this. If this is not vigorous enough when fifty, after the first month, are tried, it will be found that now this work is telling directly on the size, shape, and effectiveness of the feet and calves, and on the grace and springiness of the step itself. If any boy or girl wants to become a good jumper, or to get decided aid in learning to dance long and easily, he or she will find this a great help. If they even practice it half an hour a day, they will be none the worse for it.

All the work thus far recommended here can readily be done in two minutes. Standing erect, with the arms still akimbo, and the feet as before, now bend the knees so as to stoop six or eight inches, then rise to the perpendicular, stoop again, and continue this six times, the feet never leaving the floor. This strengthens the knees, while the front of the thighs get the heaviest part of the work, though the leg below the knee is doing a good share. (It is not unlike the exercise practised so assiduously by Rowell on the tread-mill, and which brought him such magnificent legs that he became champion pedestrian of the world.) By the third week the number may be made twenty-five. If among the scholars there are some who are decidedly weak, twenty-five of these exercises is about the limit. For strong, hearty boys, twice as many will prove nearer the mark. After two or three months of twenty-five movements as described for every day, fifty might be tried once by all the pupils, to see whether it is too severe, and if not, then maintained daily at the maximum.

Thus far the feet have not left their particular position on the floor. Now let the pupil stand with the right foot advanced about twelve or fifteen inches, suddenly rising on the toes, give a slight spring, and throw the left foot to the front, and the right back; then spring back as before, and do this six times twice a day the first week, to twelve the second, and twice as many by the end of the month. This calls the same muscles into play as the last exercise, and brings the same development, but is a little more severe and vigorous.

If still harder thigh-work is wanted, starting again, with the feet not over four inches apart, this time do not raise the heels at all, but stoop down slowly, as low as possible, bending the knees greatly, of course, the back, however, being held straight all the while. Then rise to an erect position, then go down again. Practising this three times each morning and afternoon at first, may be followed up with six a week later; and twelve by the end of the month. Better work than this for quickly giving size and strength to the thighs could hardly be devised; while, as has been already noted, scarcely any muscles on the whole body are more needed or used for ordinary walking.

Still standing erect, with arms akimbo, raise the right foot in front about as high as the left knee, keeping the right knee unbent. Hold the right foot there ten seconds; then drop it; then raise it again, fully six times. Then, standing, do the same thing with the left foot. This calls at once on the muscles across the abdomen, aiding the stomach and other vital organs there directly in their work.

This time raise the foot equally high behind; then return it to the floor and so continue, giving each foot equal work to do. The under thigh, hip, and loin are now in action; and when, later on, they become strong, their owner will find how much easier it is to run than it used to be, and also that it has become more natural to stand erect. The rate of increase of these last two exercises may be about the same as the others.

There is not much left now of the ten minutes. Still, if the work has been pushed promptly forward, there may still be a little time. However, all three of the kinds of work suggested for the front thigh need not be practised at the one recess, any one sufficing at first.

With head and neck again erect, and knees firm, hold the hands out at the sides and at arm's-length, and clasp the hands firmly together, as though trying to squeeze a rubber ball or other elastic substance. Beginning with twenty of these movements, fifty may be accomplished by the end of the fortnight; and by their continuance both the grip and the shape of the hand will be found steadily improving.

Clasp the hands together over the head. Now turn them over until the palms are upward, or turned toward the ceiling, and straighten the elbows until the hands are as high over the head as you can reach. While holding them in this position, be careful that they are not allowed to drop at all. Let the scholar march three or four times around the room in this position. It will soon be found that no apparatus whatever is necessary to get quite a large amount of exercise for the corners of the shoulders. In this way, while there is an unwonted stretching apart of the ribs, and opening up of the chest, the drawing in of the stomach and abdomen will be found to correct incipient chest weakness, half-breathing, and any tendency toward indigestion.

Following up the method, now let the class form around the side of the room, standing three feet apart, and about two feet from the wall. Place the hands against the wall, just at a level with and opposite to the shoulders. Now, keeping the heels all the time on the floor, let the body settle gradually forward until the chest touches the wall, keeping the elbows pretty near to the sides, the knees never bending a particle, and the face held upturned, the eyes looking at the ceiling directly overhead. Now push sharply off from the wall until the elbows are again straight, and the body back at vertical. Then repeat this, and continue six times for each half of the day for the first week. Keep on until you reach fifteen by the third week, and twenty-five by the second month. For expanding and deepening the chest, helping to poise the head and neck so that they will remain exactly where they belong—in an erect position —and for giving the main part of the upper back-arm quite a difficult piece of work to do, this will prove a capital exercise. Whoever will make a specialty of this one form of exercise until they daily take two or even three hundred such pushes, will find that any tendency he or she may have to flatness or hollowness of chest will soon begin to decrease, and will very likely disappear altogether.

In this last exercise most of the weight was on the feet, the hands and arms sustaining the rest. If the aisles are not over two feet and a half wide, let each pupil stand between two opposite desks and place one hand on each. Now, walking back about three or four feet, his hands still resting on the two desks, let him, keeping his body rigid and knees unbent, bend his elbows and lower his chest very gradually until it is nearly or quite level with the desk tops, then slowly straighten up his arms, and so raise his body again to the original position. Three such dips twice a day the first week, five or six the second, and by the end of the month ten or twelve, and that number then maintained steadily, will open and enlarge the chest materially before the year is out, while at the same time doing much to increase and strengthen the upper back-arm. This is harder work than pushing against the wall, because the hands and arms now have to sustain a much greater portion of the weight of the body, but it is correspondingly better for the chest.

Thus far exercises have been described calling for no apparatus at all, nor anything save a floor to stand on, a wall to push against, two ordinary school desks, and a fair degree of resolution. For children under ten, wooden dumb-bells, weighing one pound each, ought to be had of any wood-turner, and ought not to cost over five cents apiece. There might be one pair of dumb-bells given to each child, or, if the class is large, then a single dumb-bell for each, and they could be distributed among two classes for dumb-bell exercises.

Standing in the aisles, and about five feet apart, every child taking a dumb-bell in each hand, keeping the knees unbent and the head and neck erect, let them raise or "curl" the bells slowly until they are up to the shoulders, the finger-nails being held upward. Then lower, then raise again, and so on ten or twelve times each half-day for the first fortnight, and double that many thereafter. This tells principally on the biceps or front of the upper arm, on the front of the shoulder, and on the pectoral muscles, or those of the upper front chest. When, later on, any pupil endeavors to pull himself up to his chin, he will find what a large share of the work these muscles have to do. Instead of the one-pound dumb-bells then, his whole body will be the weight to be lifted.

Again, let the dumb-bells hang at the sides. Raise them slowly, high up, behind the back, keeping the elbows straight and the arms parallel. After holding them there five seconds lower them; do it again, and keep on, ten times twice a day at first, making it twenty in a fortnight, and thirty thereafter. This work will enlarge that part of the back of the upper arm next to the body, and will also tell directly on the whole back of the shoulder, and on the large muscles on the back just below where the arm joins it.

This time, holding the knuckles upward and the elbows straight, lift the dumb-bells till level with the shoulders, the arms being extended sideways as if on a cross. After holding them up five seconds, lower them; then raise them but five or six times at the first lesson, increasing to twenty by the end of the month, and then maintaining that number. The corners of the shoulders are getting the work now, and by-and-by not only shapely shoulders will come from it, but a noticeable increase of the breadth across the shoulders. This work may be varied by raising the arms parallel in front until level with the shoulders, then lowering, and so continuing.

Next raise the two bells to the shoulders; then, facing the ceiling, push both up together until they are as high over the head as possible; then lower, push up again, and continue six times twice a day for the first week; make the twelve the third week and the twenty of the fifth, and then keep at that. The outer or more noticeable parts of the upper back, the arms, are busiest now; and this exercise directly tends to enlarge and strengthen them, and to add materially to the appearance of the arms.

But one exercise more need be mentioned here. Stand erect; now draw the head and neck back of the vertical all of eight inches, until you face the ceiling. Starting with the dumb-bells high up over the head, keeping the elbows straight, lower the dumb-bells slowly, until now you are holding them at arm's-length, with your arms spread, as on a cross. Then lift them up again, lower, and continue. If this does not spread the chest open, it will be hard to find anything which will. Do this consecutively twenty times every day for a month. That number will take scarcely a minute to accomplish, but the little one-pound bells will feel wondrously heavy before the minute is over.

Here, then, have been shown quite a variety of exercises, not only safe and simple but inexpensive, which can readily be adopted in any school. If they are followed up as faithfully and steadily as are the other lessons, they cannot fail to bring decided and very welcome improvement in the shape and capacity of all the muscles, and hence of the whole body, while it will go far toward giving to all the scholars an erect and healthy carriage. These results alone would delight many a parent's heart. The making this branch of instruction as compulsory as any other would soon accustom the pupil to look for it as matter of course. If it were conducted with spirit, it would always be sure to prove interesting, and very likely to send the children back to their studies much fresher and brighter for the temporary mental rest.

Besides these exercises, the teacher, insisting on the value of an erect position in school hours, whether the pupil be standing or sitting, and by inculcating the value of this, would soon find that these efforts were being rewarded by making many a crooked girl or boy straight, and so lessening their chance of having either delicate throats or weak lungs. Care should be taken that the school chairs have broad and comfortable seats, and that the pupil never sits on a half of the seat or on the edge of it, but far back, and on the whole of it. This apparently small matter will assist marvellously in forming the habit of an erect position while sitting. Some twenty years ago a Mrs. Carman, of Boston, devised a chair-back which should just fit the hollow of the back when the back was held erect, as it should be. This simple contrivance greatly encouraged a good position in sitting, and could well be made a part of the standard chair in our schools. A pad of the right shape, hung on the back of the chair, would effect the same object.

The teacher's opportunity to work marked and permanent physical benefit to every pupil under her charge, by daily and steadily following up most or either of the above exercises, or of some substantially equivalent, can scarcely be over-estimated. The exercises strengthen the postures, whether sitting or standing. When a teacher insists on having her children erect for six hours out of the twenty-four, and makes plain to each one the value of being straight, and the self-respect it tends directly to encourage, there need be no great fear that the remaining waking hours will make any child crooked. It is in school generally that the mischief of warping and crooking is done; and hence there, of all places, would be the most appropriate place for the undoing of it.

Dumb-bells of but a pound each have been mentioned here so far. Such would be fitting for pupils under ten years of age. For all older pupils the same work with two-pound bells will prove generally vigorous enough; and whoever wishes to judge what these light weights can do in a short time should examine the results of Dr. Sargent's exercises with them and other light apparatus at Bowdoin College (see Appendix II.). Those who are already

128

decidedly strong can of course try larger bells; but it is astonishing how soon those of only two pounds seem to grow heavy, even to those who laugh at them at first.

Of course, all the work before described cannot be gone through with in ten minutes in mid-morning, or even in the twenty of the morning and afternoon sessions combined; but much of it can: and an advantage of naming too much is that it enables the teacher to vary the work from day to day, and so, while effecting the same results, prevents anything like monotony.

As the months go by, and it is found that the weaker ones have noticeably improved, and all are now capable of creditable performances at these various exercises, they may be carried safely on to the gymnasium—that is, if the school is fortunate enough to possess one. It is but a partially equipped school which is not provided with a good-sized, well-ventilated room, say of forty or fifty feet square (and one fifty by a hundred would do far better), fitted up with the simpler gymnastic appliances. Now the teacher, if up to his work, can render even more valuable assistance than before, by standing by the pupil, as he or she attempts the simplest steps on the parallel bars, or the rings, or the high bars, the pulley-weights, or the horizontal bar; constant explanations are to be given how to advance, and setting the example, detecting defects and correcting them on the spot, and all the while being ready to catch the pupil and prevent him or her from falling. An instructor soon finds that the pupils progress as rapidly as they did in the lighter preparatory work, while now they are entering on a field which, if faithfully cultivated, though for only the same brief intervals daily, will later on insure a class of strong, healthy, shapely, and symmetrical boys or girls, strong of arm and fleet of foot, familiar with what they can do, and knowing what is not to be attempted. Much, indeed the greater part, of the good to be derived from the gymnasium would have come from steadily adhering to the exercises above pointed out, so that even with no gymnasium excellent progress can be had; but results come quicker in the gymnasium, and the place invites greater freedom of action. In ten minutes in the morning, for instance, thirty or forty boys or girls could, following one another promptly, "walk" (on their hands) through the parallel bars with the elbows unbent, the head of the line crossing at once to the high bars, and "walk" or advance through them, first holding the weight on one hand and then on the other, then turning to the horizontal bar and vaulting over it. If the rear of the line is not yet through the forward "walk" on the parallels, those at the head could take a swing on the rings. Next, they could "walk" backward through the parallels, then through the high bars; then vault again, swing again, and then try the parallels anew—this time "jumping" forward, or advancing both hands at once, the arms of course being held rigidly straight. Then turning to the high bars, they could jump or advance through them, springing forward with both hands at once, vault again, the bar having meanwhile been raised, and either try the rings again or rest a moment, and then jump backward through the high bars.

A little foot-work, for a minute or two remaining, would make a good conclusion. With the hands closed and elbows bent, the body and arms held almost rigid, the neck well back, and the head up, let the column now start off around the room on an easy trot, each stepping as noiselessly as possible, and no heel touching the floor. A minute of this at a lively pace will be abundant at first; and as the legs gradually get strong, and the breathing improves, the run can be either made faster or longer, or both.

As the pupils began to grow steadier, with their hands on the bars they could next swing their feet back and forth, and jump with their hands as they swing forward; then, later, could jump forward as the feet are swung backward, and backward as the feet are swung forward. The vaulting-bar for the boys meanwhile may steadily rise, peg after peg; and, when proficiency is reached with two hands, one-hand vaulting may be tried, and the bar gradually raised as before, the teacher always standing near the vaulter. The swinging on the rings, instead of being any longer simple straight-arm work, with the body hanging nearly down, can now be done with the elbows bent much of the time, the knees being curled up toward the chin as the swinger goes backward.

After two months of straight-arm work on the parallel bars, even the girls may now try the same exercises they did with their arms when straight, save that now they should always keep them bent at the elbows. This will come hard even yet, and must be tried with care. These are the well-known "dips," followed up little by little, and month after month. By-and-by these exercises will come as easy as was the straight-arm work.

To all, or nearly all, the high bar work should now be done with bent elbows, while the vaulting should, say by the end of the year, be nearly at shoulder height for each pupil, and even, for many of them, that high with one hand. The running should have improved correspondingly, so that five minutes of it at a respectable pace, say at the rate of a mile in seven minutes, would not trouble the girls, and even ten minutes of it not distress the boys.

Now, what have these few exercises done for the muscles and their owners?

Well, the straight-arm work on the parallels, by throwing the whole weight on the hands, told directly on the upper back-arm, while the dips brought the same region into most vigorous action, and at the same time opened and strengthened the front of the chest very markedly, tending to set the shoulders back, and enlarging the chest, and hence the lung-room as well. The high-bar work told equally upon the biceps muscles, or those of the front of the upper arm, and likewise on the front of the shoulders. The vaulting made the vaulter springy, and strengthened his thighs and calves materially, and his abdominal muscles somewhat, while the more advanced work on the rings brought both the biceps and abdominal muscles into most energetic play. The running was excellent for the entire legs and the abdominals, while as a lung-expander it is difficult to equal.

Those proficient at these few exercises, if they have heeded the endeavors made to secure at all times an erect and easy carriage of the body, need but one more thing. With regular and sensible habits of eating, sleeping, dressing, and bathing, they would be almost certain to be at once well and strong. The thing wanted is daily constitutional out-of-doors exercise; whether taken afoot, on horseback, or at the oar, it matters little, so long as it is vigorously taken and faithfully persisted in, in all weathers. This guarantees that pure and bracing air shall be had, breaks up the thread of the day's thoughts, rests the mind, and quickly refits it for new work. This alone gives the full deep breathing, and the healthy tire of the muscles. It furnishes constantly varying scene, with needed eye and ear gymnastics—in short, everything which is the reverse of that quiet, sedentary, plodding life over books or papers, read too often in poorly lighted offices.

Home exercise, then, with the out-of-door life, will combine to tone us up, to invigorate our persons, and to keep off either mental or physical exhaustion and disorder.

The above work, followed up assiduously, ought to bring in its train health, symmetry, a good carriage, buoyant spirits, and a fair share of nerve and agility. But many a young man is not content with merely these; he wants to be very strong. He is already at or near his majority. He is quite strong, perhaps, in some ways, but in others is plainly deficient. What ought he to do?

Daily Exercise for Young Men.

On rising, let him stand erect, brace his chest firmly out, and, breathing deeply, curl dumb-bells (each of about one-fifteenth of his own weight) fifty times without stopping. This is biceps work enough for the early morning. Then, placing the bells on the floor at his feet, and bending his knees a little, and his arms none at all, rise to an upright position with them fifty times. The loins and back have had their turn now. After another minute's rest, standing erect, let him lift the bells fifty times as far up and out behind him as he can, keeping elbows straight, and taking care, when the bells reach the highest point behind, to hold them still there a moment. Now the under side of his arms, and about the whole of the upper back, have had their work. Next, starting with the bells at the shoulders, push them up high over the head, and lower fifty times continuously. Now the outer part of the upper arms, the corners of the shoulders, and the waist have all had active duty.

Finally, after another minute's rest, start with the bells high over the head, and lower slowly until the arms are in about the position they would be on a cross, the elbows being always kept unbent. Raise the bells to height again, then lower, and so continue until you have done ten, care being taken to hold the head six or more inches back of the perpendicular, and to steadily face the ceiling directly overhead, while the chest is swelled out to its uttermost. Rest half a minute after doing ten, then do ten more, and so on till you have accomplished fifty. This last exercise is one of the best-known chest-expanders. Now that these five sorts of work are over, few muscles above the waist have not had vigorous and ample work, the lungs themselves have had a splendid stretch, and you have not spent over fifteen minutes on the whole operation. If you want to add a little hand and forearm work, catch a broom-stick or stout cane at or near the middle, and, holding it at arm's-length, twist it rapidly from side to side a hundred times with one hand, and then with the other.

In the late afternoon a five-mile walk on the road, at a four-mile pace, with the step inclined to be short, the knees bent but little, and the foot pushing harder than usual as it leaves the ground—this will be found to bring the legs and loins no inconsiderable exercise; all, in fact, that they will probably need. If, shortly before bedtime each evening, the youth, after he has been working as above, say for a month, will, in light clothes and any old and easy shoes, run a mile in about seven minutes and a half, and, a little later, under the seven minutes, or, three nights a week, make the distance two miles each night, there will soon be a life and vigor in his legs which used to be unknown; and if six months of this work brings a whole inch more on thigh and calf, it is only what might have been expected.

For still more rapid and decided advance, an hour at the gymnasium during the latter part of the morning, half of it at the rowing-weights, so thickening and stoutening the back, and the other half at "dipping" and other half-arm work on the parallel bars—so spreading and enlarging the chest and stoutening the back-arms—these will increase the development rapidly, and will sharpen the appetite at a corresponding rate. But it must be real work, and no dawdling or time lost.

Few young men in any active employment, however, can spare this morning hour. Still, without it, if they will follow up the before-breakfast work, the walking in the fashion named, and the running, they will soon find time enough for this much, and most satisfactory results in the way of improved health and increased strength as well. Indeed, it will for most young men prove about the right amount to keep them toned up and ready for their day's work. If they desire great development in any special line, let them select some of the exercises described in the previous chapter, as aimed to effect such development, and practice them as assiduously, if need be, as Rowell did his tread-mill work for his legs.

Daily Exercise for Women.

And what should the girls and women do each day? With two-pound wooden dumb-bells at first, let them, before breakfast, go through twenty-five movements of each of the five sorts just described for young men. After six weeks or two months they can increase the number to fifty, and, if this does not bring the desired increase in size, and strength of arm and chest and back, then they can try dumb-bells weighing four or five pounds each.

Out-of-doors, either in the latter part of the morning or afternoon, if they will, in broad, easy shoes, walk for one hour, not at any listless two-mile pace, but at first as fast as they comfortably can, and then gradually increasing until in a fortnight or more they can make sure of three miles and a half at least, if not of four miles within the hour, and will observe the way of stepping just suggested to the men, they will get about walking enough. And if once in awhile, every Saturday, for instance, they make the walk all of five or six miles, getting, if city ladies, quite out into the suburbs and back, they will be surprised and gratified at the greater ease with which they can walk now than formerly, and at their freshness at the end. Recent reports from India say that English ladies there often spend two or three hours daily in the saddle. Every American lady who can manage to ride that much, or half of it, and at a strong, brisk pace, will soon have a health and vigor almost unknown among our women and girls to-day.

If walking and horseback parties, instead of being, as now, well-nigh unheard of among our girls, were every-day affairs, and there was not a point of interest within ten miles which every girl, and woman too, did not know well, it would prove a benefit both to them and to the next generation which would be almost incalculable.

Girls should also learn to run. Few of them are either easy or graceful runners; but it is an accomplishment quickly learned; and begun at a short distance and slow jog, and continued until the girl thinks nothing of running a mile in seven minutes, and that without once touching a heel to the ground, it will do more than almost any other known exercise to make her graceful and easy on her feet, and also to enlarge and strengthen her lungs. A roomy school-yard, a bit of lawn, or a gymnasium-track, either of these is all the place needed in which to learn this now almost obsolete accomplishment. The gymnasium is perhaps the best place, as there they can wear costumes which do not impede freedom of movement.

If besides these things the girl or woman will determine that, as much as possible of the time each day in which she is sitting down, she will sit with head and neck up, trunk erect, and with shoulders low, and that whenever she stands or walks she will at all times be upright, she will shortly find that she is getting to be far straighter than she was, and, if she has a larger and finer chest than formerly, it will be nothing strange, for she has simply been using one of the means to get it. If a still greater variety of daily work is desired, she can select it from Chapter XII.; the exercises on the pulley-weights and on the apparatus sketched in Fig. 8 being especially desirable.

Daily Exercise for Business Men.

And what daily work shall the business man take? His aim is not to lay on muscle, not to become equal to this or that athletic feat, but simply to so exercise as to keep his entire physical and mental machinery in good working order, and himself equal to all demands likely to be made on him.

First he, like the young man or the woman, should make sure of the ten or fifteen minutes' work before breakfast. Not through the long day again will he be likely to have another good opportunity for physical exercise, at least until evening, and then he will plead that he is too tired. But in the early morning, fresh and rested, and with a few minutes at his disposal, he can, as Bryant did, without serious or violent effort, work himself great benefit, the good effect of which will stay by him all the day. If he has in his room the few bits of apparatus suggested in the chapter on "Home Gymnasiums," he will be better off than Bryant was, in that he can have a far wider range of exercise, and that all ready at hand.

Let him first devote two or three minutes to the striking-bag. Facing it squarely, with head back and chest well out, let him strike it a succession of vigorous blows, with left and right fists alternating, until he has done a hundred in all. If he has hit hard and with spirit, he is puffing freely now, his lungs are fully expanded, his legs have had a deal of springing about to do, and his arms and chest have been busiest of all. This bag-work is really superb exercise, and if once or twice, later in the day, say at one's place of business, or at home again in the evening, he would take some more of it, he would find fret, discomfort, and indigestion flying to the winds, and in their place buoyancy and exhilaration of spirits to which too many men have long been strangers.

Next grasp the handles in Fig. 8 and bear downward, as described on page 249. Repeat this work for about two minutes, standing all the time thoroughly erect. Whether the sparring left any part of your chest unfilled or not, every air-cell is expanded now, while you cannot fail to be pleased with the thorough way in which this simple contrivance does its work. Care should of course be taken that the air breathed during these exercises is pure and fresh.

Now use the dumb-bells two or three minutes. Let them weigh not over one twenty-fifth of your own weight. First, with head and neck a trifle back of vertical, and the chest held out as full as possible, curl the bells, or lift them from down at arm's-length until you have drawn them close up to the shoulders, the finger-nails being turned upward. Lower again and repeat until you have done twenty-five, the chest being always out. The biceps muscles, or those of the front upper arm, and of the front of the shoulders and chest, have been busy now.

Next, starting with the bells at your shoulders, push both at once steadily up over your head as high as you can reach, and continue till twenty-five are accomplished. The back-arms, corners of the shoulders, and the waist have now had their turn.

Facing the pulley-weights (Fig. 4), and standing about two feet from them, catch a handle in each hand. Keeping the elbows stiff, draw first one hand and then the other in a horizontal line until your hand is about eighteen inches behind you, the body and legs being at all times held rigidly erect, and the chest well out. Continue this until you have done fifty strokes with each hand. This is excellent for the back of the shoulders—indeed for nearly the entire back above the waist.

Again, with back to the pulley-weights, hold the handles high over the head, and leaning forward about a foot, keeping the elbows unbent, bear the handles directly downward in front of you, and so do twenty-five.

Besides these few things, or most of them, put the bar (Fig. 3) in the upper place, and, catching it with both hands, just swing back and forth, at first for half a minute, afterward longer, always holding the head well back. This is capital at stretching the ribs apart and expanding the chest. If the above exercises seem too hard at first, begin with half as much, or even less, and work gradually up until the number named can be easily done.

If, once in mid-morning and again in mid-afternoon, the man, right in his store or office, will turn for two or three minutes to his dumb-bells, and repeat what he did with his home pair in the morning, he will find the rest and change most refreshing. But in any case, whether he does so or not, *every man in this country whose life is in-door ought to so divide his time that, come what may, he will make sure of his hour out-of-doors in the late afternoon, when the day's work is nearly or quite done.* If he must get up earlier, or get to his work earlier, or work faster while he does work, no matter. The prize is well worth any such sacrifice, and even five times it. Emerson well says, "The first wealth is health," and no pains should be spared to secure it. Lose it awhile and see. Exercise vigorously that hour afoot, or horseback, or on the water, making sure that during it you utterly ignore your business and usual thoughts. Walk less at first, but soon do your four miles in the hour, and then stick to that, of course having shoes in which it is easy to walk, and before long the good appetite of boyhood will return, food taste as it often has not done for years, sound sleep will be surer, and new life and zest will be infused into all that you do. Let every man in this country who lives by brain-work get this daily "constitutional" at all hazards, and it will do more to secure to him future years of health and usefulness than almost anything else he can do. It will be observed that there is nothing severe or violent in any of these exercises suggested for men—nothing that old or young may not take with like advantage. The whole idea is to point out a plain and simple plan of exercise, which, followed up faithfully, will make sound health almost certain, and which is easily within the reach of all.

Daily Exercise for Consumptives.

And what should these people do? If there is one good lung left, or a goodly portion of two, there is much which they can do. Before breakfast they need to be more careful than others because of their poorer circulation. Still, in a warm and comfortable room they can work to advantage even then. In most instances consumptives have not large enough chests. Stripped to the waist, there is found to be a flatness of the upper chest, a lack of depth straight through from breastbone to spine; and the girth about the chest itself, and especially at the lower part of it, is often two or more inches less than it is in a well-built person of the same height. Now, to weed out these defects, to swell up and enlarge the chest, and bring it proper breadth, and depth, and fulness, this will go far toward insuring healthy and vigorous lungs. And how is this done?

Standing under the handles in an appliance like that represented in Fig. 8, holding the body rigidly erect, the chest out, the knees and elbows unbent, bear the two handles downward on either side of you until the hands are as if extended on a cross, using only very light weights at first. Lower the weights again, then bear down again, and so do ten. Just as you bear down each time, inflate the lungs to their utmost, and hold the air in them until you have lowered the weights again. Rest about a minute, then do ten more, and a little later ten more. This will be enough before breakfast work the first week. At breakfast, and whenever sitting down throughout the day, determine to do two things—to sit far back on your chair, and to sit at all times upright. No matter how many times you forget or fail, even if a thousand, keep trying until the erect posture becomes habitual. This point once reached, you have accomplished a great thing—one which may aid not a little to save your life.

Next, about an hour after breakfast, start out for an easy walk. Going quietly at first, the head held, if anything, back of the vertical, and the step short and springy; quicken later into a lively pace, and, holding that as long as you comfortably can, return to your room. If your skin is moist, do not hesitate a minute, but strip at once, and with coarse towels rub your skin till it is thoroughly red all over, and then put on dry under-clothing. If you then feel like taking a nap, take it. When well rested, do thirty more strokes at the pulley-weights. In the afternoon try more walking, or some horseback work if you can get a steed with any dash in him. After you are through, then more weight work. Finally, just before retiring, take another turn at the weights.

After the first week run the weight work up to fifty at a time, and increase the out-door distance covered both morning and afternoon, being sure to go in all weathers, and to eat and sleep all you comfortably can. Vary the in-door work also somewhat. In addition to the exercise on Fig. 8, practice now an equal number of strokes daily on the appliance described as Fig. 9, and in the fashion described on page 249. After the first fortnight try hanging by the two hands on the horizontal bar and swinging lightly back and forth. Before breakfast, before dinner, before supper, and just before retiring, take a turn at this swinging. Of it, and the work on the two sorts of pulley-weights, a weak-lunged person can scarcely do enough. These open the ribs apart, broaden and deepen the chest, and inflate the lungs—the very things the consumptive needs. The out-door work secures him or her ample good air, vigorous exercise, and frequent change of scene. On the value of this good air, or rather of the danger of bad air, hear Langenbeck, the great German anatomist: "I am sure now of what I suspected long ago, viz., that pulmonary diseases have very little to do with intemperance, * * * and much less with cold weather, but are nearly exclusively (if we except tuberculous tendencies inherited from *both* parents, I say *quite* exclusively) produced by the breathing of foul air." This out-door work should also be steadily increased until the half-hour's listless walk at first becomes six or eight miles before dinner, and as much more before supper. From breakfast to supper one can hardly be exercising out-of-doors too much; and steadily calling on the heart and lungs in these very favorable ways, increased vigor and power are only what might have reasonably been looked for.

As the months roll on, and this steady work, directed right to the weak spots, has strengthened and toughened you, now put larger weights on the Fig. 8 appliance, and also increase the number of strokes until you do a thousand or even two thousand daily—head and body always being held erect, and full breathing a constant accompaniment. This making a specialty of these chest-expanding exercises, none of which are severe or violent, but which are still vigorous enough, and the abundance of healthy and active out-door life, are sure to bring good fruits in this battle where the stake is no less than one's own life. They are rational and vigorous means, aimed directly at the weak part, and, with good air, good food, cheerful friends, and ample sleep, will often work marvels, where the filling the stomach with a whole apothecary shop of nauseous oils and other medicines has wholly failed to bring the relief sought. These exercises taken by a man already healthy at once tone him up and invigorate him, until he begins to have something of the feeling of the sturdy pioneer, as described by Dr. Mitchell.[P] And if the delicate person tries the same means, using them judiciously and carefully, it is but natural that he should find similar results.

Some years ago Dr. G——, of Boston, showed us a photograph of himself taken several years previously. The shoulders were warped forward, the chest looked flat, almost hollow, and the face and general appearance suggested a delicate man. He said he inclined to be consumptive. Well, by practising breathing, not on an ordinary "blowing-machine," where you empty your lungs of about all that is in them, but on an inspirometer, from which instead you inhale every inch of air you can, and by practising vigorous working of his diaphragm, he had so expanded his lungs that he could inhale three hundred and eighty cubic inches of air at one breath! Certainly the depth of his chest at the later period was something astounding, it being, as nearly as we could judge without calipers, all of fourteen inches through, directly from breastbone to spine, while it was a strikingly broad chest as well.

But an even more astonishing feature was the tremendous power of his voice. He said that at the end of half an hour's public singing with the opera singers (for he was skilled at that), while they would be hot and perspiring he was only just warming up and getting ready for his work. One thing all who ever heard him sing would quickly concede, namely, that seldom had they anywhere heard so immense a voice as his. He said that he had also run two blocks in one breath. He looked about the farthest remove from a consumptive—a short, stout, fat man, rather.

Now the in-door chest work above recommended, and the steady and vigorous daily out-door work, all aiming to deepen and strengthen the lungs, are well-nigh sure to bring decidedly favorable results; while the doctor's habit of frequent, deep, and slow inhaling, cannot fail to work great good, and can hardly be practised enough.

After he of weak lungs has once built them up again and regained the former vigor, he should not only be sure of his daily in-door exercise and of his constitutional, but of a longer outing daily than a stronger man would need. President Day, of Yale, said to have been a consumptive at seventeen, by good care of his body lived to be ninety-five, and it is far from uncommon for delicate persons, who take good care of the small stock of vigor they have, to outlive sturdier ones who are more prodigal and careless.

APPENDIX I.

Showing the average state of the development of 200 men upon entering the Bowdoin College Gymnasium, from the classes of '73, '74, '75, '76, and '77.

Age		18.3 years.
Height	5 ft. 8 in.	67.974 in.
Weight	135 lbs.	134.981 lbs.
Chest (inflated.)	35 in.	35.067 in.
Chest (contracted)	32$\frac{1}{4}$ in.	32.29 in.
Forearm	10 in.	10.03 in.
Upper arm (flexed)	11 in.	10.960 in.
Shoulders (width)	15$\frac{1}{2}$ in.	15.602 in.
Hips	31$\frac{1}{2}$ in.	31.475 in.
Thigh	19$\frac{1}{2}$ in.	19.612 in.
Calf	12$\frac{1}{2}$ in.	12.729 in.

APPENDIX II.

Showing the average state of the growth and development of the same number of men (200) after having practised in the Bowdoin Gymnasium half an hour a day *four times a week, for a period of six months, under Dr. Sargent.*

Height	5 ft. 8¹/₄ in.	68.254 in.
Weight	137 lbs.	137.123 lbs.
Chest (inflated)	36¹/₄ in.	36.829 in.
Chest (contracted)	33 in.	33.206 in.
Forearm	10³/₄ in.	10.760 in.
Upper arm (flexed)	12 in.	11.903 in.
Shoulders (width)	16¹/₄ in.	16.260 in.
Hips	33³/₄ in.	33.875 in.
Thigh	21 in.	20.964 in.
Calf	13¹/₄ in.	13.232 in.

In this case the apparatus used was light dumb-bells, 2½ lbs.; Indian clubs, 3½ lbs.; pulley-weights, from 10 to 15 lbs.

APPENDIX III.

Showing average increase of 200 students at Bowdoin College, in various measurements, after working but half an hour a day four times a week, for six months, under Dr. Sargent.

Average increase in height	$1/4$ in.
Average increase in weight	2 lbs.
Average increase of chest (contracted)	$3/4$ in.
Average increase of chest (inflated)	$1\,3/4$ in.
Average increase of girth of forearm	$3/4$ in.
Average increase of girth of upper arm	1 in.
Average increase of width of shoulders	$3/4$ in.
Average increase of girth of hips	$2\,1/4$ in.
Average increase of girth of thigh	$1\,1/2$ in.
Average increase of girth of calf	$3/4$ in.

APPENDIX IV.

Showing the effect of four hours' exercise a week for one year upon a youth of 19, at Bowdoin College, under Dr. Sargent's direction. This was two hours' work more each week than was required of the regular classes.

S——.	Age.	Height.		Weight.	Ches (infl).	Ches (cont.).	Fore arm.	Upp'r arm.	Shoulders.	Hips.	Thigh.	Calf.
Date.	Yrs.	Ft.	In.	Lbs.	In.	In.	In.	In.	In.	In.	In.	In.
Nov., '73	19	5	8	145	$36\frac{1}{2}$	$33\frac{1}{2}$	$10\frac{1}{4}$	$12\frac{1}{4}$	$15\frac{3}{4}$	35	$19\frac{3}{4}$	$13\frac{1}{2}$
Nov., '74	20	5	9	160	40	$34\frac{1}{4}$	11	$13\frac{3}{4}$	17	$36\frac{1}{2}$	22	15
Increase			1	15	$3\frac{1}{2}$	$\frac{3}{4}$	$\frac{3}{4}$	$1\frac{1}{2}$	$1\frac{1}{4}$	$1\frac{1}{2}$	$2\frac{1}{4}$	$1\frac{1}{2}$

APPENDIX V.

Taken from Maclaren's "Physical Education." Showing effect of four months and twelve days' exercise, under his system, on fifteen youths ranging from 16 to 19 years of age.

RETURN OF COURSE OF GYMNASTIC TRAINING AT THE ROYAL MILITARY ACADEMY, WOOLWICH, FROM FEB. 10TH, 1863, TO JUNE 22D, 1863.

No.	Age	Height		Weight		Chest	Fore arm	Upper arm	Height	Weight	Chest	Fore arm	Upper arm
						MEASUREMENTS, ETC.					INCREASE.		
	Yrs.	Ft.	In.	St.	Lbs.	In.	In.	In.	In.	Lbs.	In.	In.	In.
1	18	5	$1\frac{1}{4}$	7	8	$29\frac{1}{2}$	$9\frac{1}{2}$	$8\frac{3}{4}$					
		5	$2\frac{1}{4}$	7	8	30	$9\frac{1}{2}$	$9\frac{1}{2}$	1	"	$\frac{1}{2}$	"	$\frac{3}{4}$
2	19	5	$8\frac{1}{2}$	9	$5\frac{1}{2}$	28	11	$10\frac{1}{4}$					
		5	$8\frac{3}{4}$	9	11	$31\frac{1}{2}$	11	$11\frac{3}{8}$	$\frac{1}{4}$	$5\frac{1}{2}$	$3\frac{1}{2}$	"	$1\frac{1}{8}$
3	17	5	$5\frac{3}{4}$	9	1	$26\frac{1}{2}$		$8\frac{1}{2}$					
		5	$6\frac{1}{8}$	9	1	$29\frac{1}{2}$	$10\frac{3}{8}$	10	$\frac{3}{8}$	"	3	"	$1\frac{1}{2}$
4	18	5	$8\frac{1}{4}$	10	0	33	$10\frac{3}{8}$	$10\frac{1}{4}$					
		5	$8\frac{1}{2}$	10	3	35	$10\frac{3}{8}$	$11\frac{1}{2}$	$\frac{1}{4}$	3	2	"	$1\frac{1}{4}$
5	18	6	$0\frac{1}{2}$	10	13	32	$10\frac{1}{2}$	$9\frac{1}{4}$					
		6	$1\frac{1}{4}$	11	2	34	$10\frac{1}{2}$	$10\frac{7}{8}$	$\frac{3}{4}$	3	2	"	$1\frac{5}{8}$
6	17	5	$3\frac{1}{2}$	8	1	31	$10\frac{1}{8}$	$9\frac{7}{8}$					
		5	$4\frac{1}{2}$	8	7	33	$10\frac{1}{8}$	11	1	6	2	"	$1\frac{1}{8}$
7	18	5	$5\frac{1}{4}$	7	13	26	$9\frac{1}{4}$	$7\frac{7}{8}$					
		5	$5\frac{1}{4}$	8	2	29	$9\frac{1}{2}$	$9\frac{1}{2}$	$\frac{1}{2}$	3	3	$\frac{1}{4}$	$1\frac{5}{8}$
8	16	5	$6\frac{1}{4}$	8	3	$28\frac{1}{2}$	9	$8\frac{1}{2}$					
		5	$7\frac{1}{4}$	8	4	31	$9\frac{7}{8}$	$9\frac{1}{2}$	$\frac{1}{2}$	1	$2\frac{1}{2}$	$\frac{1}{8}$	1
9	17	5	$8\frac{3}{8}$	11	3	31	$11\frac{1}{4}$	$10\frac{1}{4}$					
		5	$9\frac{1}{4}$	11	3	33	$11\frac{1}{4}$	$11\frac{1}{4}$	$\frac{3}{4}$	"	2	"	$\frac{7}{8}$
10	18	5	$11\frac{3}{8}$	11	8	30	$10\frac{1}{4}$	$10\frac{1}{2}$					
		5	$11\frac{3}{8}$	11	8	33	$10\frac{3}{4}$	11	"	"	3	$\frac{1}{2}$	$\frac{1}{2}$
11	19	5	$7\frac{3}{4}$	10	2	33	$10\frac{1}{2}$	$10\frac{1}{4}$					
		5	$8\frac{5}{8}$	10	2	$34\frac{1}{2}$	$10\frac{1}{2}$	$10\frac{7}{8}$	$\frac{7}{8}$	"	$1\frac{1}{2}$	"	$\frac{5}{8}$

12	18	5	$10^1/_2$	10	11	32	$10^1/_2$	10					
		5	$11^7/_8$	10	11	$33^1/_2$	$10^1/_2$	11	$1^3/_8$	"	$1^1/_2$	"	1
13	19	5	$7^7/_8$	11	13	33	$11^1/_2$	12					
		5	$9^5/_8$	11	13	$35^1/_2$	$11^1/_2$	$12^1/_2$	$1^3/_4$	"	$2^1/_2$	"	$^1/_2$
14	17	5	$6^1/_4$	9	13	29	$10^5/_8$	$8^1/_4$					
		5	$7^5/_8$	10	3	32	$10^5/_8$	$9^1/_2$	$^7/_8$	4	3	"	$^1/_4$
15	19	5	$10^1/_8$	10	1	$27^1/_2$	$10^5/_8$	$9^5/_8$					
		5	$11^7/_8$	10	9	$32^3/_4$	$10^5/_8$	$10^7/_8$	$1^3/_4$	8	$5^1/_4$	"	$1^1/_2$

APPENDIX VI.

Taken from Maclaren's "Physical Education." Showing effect of seven months and nineteen days' exercise, under his system, on men ranging from 19 to 28 years of age.

TABLE OF MEASUREMENTS OF FIRST DETACHMENT OF NON-COMMISSIONED OFFICERS SELECTED TO BE QUALIFIED AS MILITARY GYMNASTIC INSTRUCTORS.

			MEASUREMENTS, Etc.							INCREASE.				
Date	No	Age.	Height.		Weight.		Chest	Forearm	Upper arm.	Height	Weight	Chest	Forearm	Upper arm.
		Yrs.	Ft.	In.	St.	Lbs.	In.	In.	In.	In.	Lbs.	In.	In.	In.
Sept. 11.	1	19	5	$8^1/_2$	9	2	33	$9^1/_2$	10					
April 30.			5	$8^7/_8$	10	1	$37^1/_2$	$10^1/_2$	$11^3/_4$	$^3/_8$	13	$4^1/_2$	1	$1^3/_4$
Sept. 11.	2	21	5	9	10	5	$34^3/_4$	10	11					
April 30.			5	$9^1/_4$	11	1	$38^1/_2$	11	$12^1/_4$	$^1/_4$	10	$3^3/_4$	1	$1^1/_4$
Sept 11.	3	23	5	5	9	7	34	$10^1/_2$	12					
April 30.			5	$5^3/_4$	10	2	$37^1/_4$	$11^1/_4$	$13^1/_4$	$^3/_4$	9	$3^1/_4$	1	$1^1/_4$
Sept. 11.	4	23	5	$7^1/_4$	9	13	37	$10^1/_4$	12					
April 30.			5	$7^3/_4$	10	8	$38^1/_2$	$11^1/_2$	13	$^1/_2$	9	$1^1/_2$	$1^1/_4$	1
Sept. 11.	5	23	5	$8^1/_4$	9	10	36	10	11					
April 30.			5	$8^1/_2$	10	6	37	$10^1/_2$	12	$^1/_4$	10	1	$^1/_2$	1
Sept. 11.	6	23	5	$9^1/_8$	11	3	$36^1/_2$	11	12					
April 30.			5	$9^1/_4$	11	12	$38^1/_2$	$11^1/_2$	13	$^1/_8$	9	2	$^1/_2$	1
Sept. 11.	7	23	5	9	10	6	36	$10^3/_4$	12					
April 30.			5	$9^1/_8$	10	11	$38^1/_2$	11	13	$^1/_8$	5	$2^1/_2$	$^1/_4$	1
Sept. 11.	8	24	5	$8^3/_4$	10	8	35	$10^3/_4$	$12^3/_4$					
April 30.			5	$9^1/_4$	11	6	40	$11^3/_4$	14	$^1/_2$	12	5	1	$1^1/_4$
Sept. 11.	9	26	5	$6^1/_4$	9	5	33	10	$11^1/_2$					

April 30.			5	$6\frac{1}{8}$	9	$11\frac{1}{2}$	36	$10\frac{1}{4}$	$12\frac{1}{4}$	$\frac{5}{8}$	$6\frac{1}{2}$	3	$\frac{1}{4}$	$1\frac{1}{4}$
Sept. 11.	10	$26\frac{3}{4}$	5	$11\frac{1}{8}$	12	6	41	$11\frac{1}{2}$	13					
April 30.			5	$11\frac{3}{4}$	13	1	42	$11\frac{1}{2}$	14	$\frac{3}{8}$	9	1	"	1
Sept. 11.	11	28	5	$7\frac{1}{4}$	10	10	37	$10\frac{1}{2}$	$12\frac{1}{2}$					
April 30.			5	$8\frac{1}{4}$	11	9	40	$11\frac{1}{4}$	$13\frac{3}{4}$	$\frac{1}{2}$	13	3	$1\frac{1}{4}$	$1\frac{1}{4}$
Sept. 11.	12	28	5	$10\frac{7}{8}$	10	9	37	$10\frac{1}{4}$	13					
April 30.			5	11	11	11	40	$1\frac{3}{4}$	14	$\frac{1}{8}$	16	3	$1\frac{1}{4}$	1

The men composing this detachment had been irregularly selected, the youngest being 19, the eldest 28, the average age 24; and, after a period of *eight months'* training, the increase in the measurements of the men were—

	Weight.	Chest.	Forearm.	Upper arm.
	Lbs.	In.	In.	In.
The smallest gain	5	1	$\frac{1}{4}$	1
The largest gain	16	5	$1\frac{1}{4}$	$1\frac{3}{4}$
The average gain	10	$2\frac{7}{8}$	$\frac{3}{4}$	$1\frac{3}{4}$

APPENDIX VII.

Taken from Maclaren's "Physical Education." Showing the result of one year's continuous practice.

THE FOLLOWING TABLE SHOWS IN ANOTHER FORM THE RESULTS OF THE SYSTEM; NOT BY BRIEF COURSES OR PERIODS OF VOLUNTARY ATTENDANCE, BUT BY A YEAR'S STEADY PRACTICE FROM BIRTHDAY TO BIRTHDAY, WITH TWO ARTICLED PUPILS, THE YOUNGER BEING 16, THE ELDER 20:

			MEASUREMENTS, ETC.							INCREASE.				
Case.	Date.	Age.	Height.		Weight.		Chest.	Forearm.	Upper arm.	Height.	Weight.	Chest.	Forearm.	Upper arm.
		Yrs.	Ft.	In.	St.	Lbs.	In.	In.	In.	In.	Lbs.	In.	In.	In.
A.	1861, Oct. 17.	16	5	$2^3/_4$	7	10	31	8	$9^1/_4$					
	1862, Apr. 17.	"	5	4	8	12	$34^1/_2$	10	$11^1/_4$	$1^1/_4$	16	$3^1/_2$	2	2
	" Oct. 17.	17	5	$4^3/_4$	9	3	36	10	$11^1/_4$	$^3/_4$	5	$1^1/_2$	"	"
							Subsequent Measurement.							
	1863, Mar. 23.	18	5	$6^3/_8$	10	10	$37^1/_2$	$11^1/_4$	13	$1^5/_8$	21	$1^1/_2$	$1^1/_4$	$1^3/_4$
B.	1862, Feb. 24.	20	5	$8^1/_2$	10	13	34	$11^1/_4$	$11^3/_4$					
	" Aug. 24.	"	5	$8^7/_8$	11	4	$38^1/_2$	12	$12^1/_4$	$^3/_8$	5	$4^1/_2$	$^3/_4$	1
	1862, Feb. 24.	21	"		11	$7^1/_2$	40	$12^1/_2$	$13^1/_4$	"	$3^1/_2$	$1^1/_2$	$^1/_2$	$^1/_2$

Thus in the year's work the increase was—

Upper

	Height.	Weight.	Chest.	Forearm.	arm.
	In.	Lbs.	In.	In.	In.
With the younger	2	21	5	2	2
With the elder	$^3/_8$	$8^1/_2$	6	$1^1/_4$	$1^1/_2$

CONCLUSION.

In the first eleven chapters of this little book attempt has been made to call attention both to defects and lacks, resulting largely from not taking rational daily exercise, and to what such exercise has accomplished wherever it has been thoroughly tried. In the last two chapters have been suggested not a long and difficult system of gymnastic exercises needing a fully equipped gymnasium, a trained instructor, and years of work to master, but rather a few plain and simple exercises for any given part or for the whole body, and hints as to how to distribute the little time to be given to them daily. The teacher, the parent—the child even, without the aid of either—the young man or woman, the middle-aged and the old, will all find variety enough of work, which, while free from risk, will still prove sufficiently vigorous to insure to each a good allowance of daily exercise. All else that is needed is a good degree of the steadiness and perseverance which are generally inseparable from everything worth accomplishing.

THE END.